DIARY OF AN ULIKELY HERO
BATTLE TO SAVE MINECRAFT

Book 1

By Axel Silverblade

TABLE OF CONTENT

DAY 1

Good morning diary.

And what a beautiful morning it is in Jebville. The cubic sun rises slowly over the town, a soft orange glow basking structures of wood and stone. Humans and villagers mill between the buildings, setting about their daily tasks. The town guard watches the west with a steely resolve, sword sharpened in case they need to marry their blades in violent ceremony.

Jebville in all its glory...

Not that it'll ever happen. There hasn't been a mob attack in over a decade. All is as it should be.

It occurs to me I should probably introduce myself. Which is kind of weird. I already know who I am, and I'm pretty sure my diary has no need for my name. Well, I mean if I ever lose it then it'll make it much easier to return the book.

The name's Axel. I know, the name rocks. I work as the local librarian here in Jebville. My tasks include organizing the books, cataloging books that get delivered and, when things get exciting, finding books for people. Sometimes they'll give me the title, other times they'll only know the color of the book. Either way, it's always a worthy challenge for someone like myself. Some slay hordes of aberrations, but I smite down illiteracy.

It's been a while since I owned a diary. Haven't had one since the seventh grade, when Chad Fireblast invited half the school to his parent's place for a big summer bash. During which, he proceeded to procure my diary and read my deepest, darkest secrets in front of my classmates. From my crushes to my dreams of being a Dragon Slayer.

Yeah, I slammed the breaks on that dream pretty quickly.

Well just look at me now Chad. I'm the head librarian. What do you have? Nothing. Except for your dad's millions of emeralds, massive mansions, cushy jobs, decked-out Minecarts and- Okay so he's got all of that, but aside from that what does he really have? That's right, nothing.

Life problems aside, I'm not even sure why I bought this. Was it just to document my life? Was it maybe to write the first of a bestselling series of books? Or is it because my life is about to undergo an incredible transformation, in which I shall finally fulfill my crushed childhood dream of becoming the hero of the world?

Haha, nope. Not now, not ever.

DAY 2

Another great day of librarianing.

It's not much, but I love it here.

Is that even a word? Eh, whatever, I'll sneak it into the dictionary next time I'm at work...

I mean, I won't. I wouldn't dare besmirch a book in such a fashion. I'm not some awful Pillager.

At any rate, it wasn't much of an eventful day, diary. A slow burner, even for a shift at the library. Very few people popped in looking to borrow books. I had one guy come in thinking he could buy books at the library.

Hah. Yeah right. But aside from that brief bit of excitement, nothing to report.

Oh wait, there was one thing. Looks like we've got a LARPing convention in town. A bunch of dressed-up figures has been showing up in town. Some of them in full armor, others clad in magical robes. Fun hobby, but too exciting for someone like me. Still, they're really good at it. Some of them look like famous Minecraft heroes. Trueshot the Archer, Phalanx the Spearmaster and even Bob the Undefeated.

Can't possibly be them though. We haven't seen a hero in this town for years.

DAY 3

Had another one of the fanboys visit me today.

Honestly, it can get quite embarrassing at times. I work hard to keep myself hidden from others, to keep my privacy intact. I'd go so far as to get my name changed if it weren't for the fact that I get asked for autographs every time I try to visit the government building. But whatever, something you must live with when you're descended from such a proud lineage.

Huh, I don't think I ever mentioned that before. Alright, lemme explain.

I am Axel Silverblade, son of Typhon Silverblade who was the son of Blake Silverblade, who just so happened to be the son of Shade Silverblade. Some of the edgiest names around, I know. It's a tradition in the family. What you might not realize is that Silverblades are destined for greatness.

Take my father for instance. He was the man who slew the Ender Dragon. Single-handed. I'm told it was a truly epic battle which destroyed half of The End. Told, of course, because no one was there to witness it. He just emerged from the portal afterward, carrying a giant dragon head and rode off into the distance, seeking his next adventure.

Blake Silverblade did something even cooler. He decided he wanted to take an expedition to the Nether. He packed enough supplies for about a week and then set off through the portal. His family didn't see him again for about two years. They figured he'd died and even held a funeral for him. Except one day he showed up back home and proclaimed to have mapped out almost the entire Nether. He also stated he took over a bunch of fortresses, slew hundreds of Blazes, rode atop a Ghast and even created a water supply. In the Nether. Y'know, where it evaporates instantly?

And finally, we have Shade Silverblade. He's renowned, even among his own family.

You see, back in the day, there was a group of Minecrafters with some... weird powers. They could create any block they so wished, fly around at lightning speeds, teleport across the world and even kill players with a snap of their fingers. Oh, and they were also invincible. Shade Silverblade somehow managed to beat them all, stripped them of their powers and sealed them away in a dark dungeon.

Long story short, my family is incredibly famous. Something I despise because I don't want to be famous.

I like working away in my little library. I like stacking shelves, reading books, sweeping the floors, writing books, sometimes sneaking away for a bowl of soup and above all else, I like the quiet. It is magnificent. No noises, no screaming and yelling, just peace and relaxation.

At least until someone finds out a Silverblade works here and they rush over for an autograph and a selfie. It's gotten to the point where everybody who wants a photo needs to sign a contract, promising they will never reveal where I work. Most of the time they just leave and never come back. Whatever. Suits me just fine.

...

I suppose I should explain why I don't want to be recognized.

People place expectations on you when your family is famous. They want to know what you'll do to uphold the legacy or continue their great work. Me? I don't plan on adventuring or fighting monsters or spending years in the Nether. I don't want to. It's never appealed to me, and I know I wouldn't be good at it. I can't shoot a bow or hold a sword properly, but I'm expected to go fight the forces of darkness? No thanks.

Besides, the era of adventurers is over. Mobs are a thing of the past, and both the Nether and the End have been conquered. There's not a desert temple nor underwater fortress which remains unlooted, and griefers don't have the power to challenge the heroes of the world. So even if I wanted to do something, there'd be no point.

Long live the era of the librarian!

DAY 4

I... okay, today has been a strange day. I'm gonna write it all down and see if I can't make sense of everything.

Two weird things happened today. The first was in the early morning. I'd just opened the library and was stacking some books when a skulking figure entered. Draped in black capes and robes, he twitched every few seconds and constantly looked over his shoulder.

"Excuse me, can I help you?" I asked him.

"Nhh," he grunted at me, before closing the shop door. He motioned for me to be quiet, and I started wondering if there was some LARPing convention in town.

"Are you looking for something?" I prodded again.

"BE SILENT!" He cursed at me, spittle running from his lips. He placed a dirty, gloved hand across my mouth and made sure I said nothing more. I rolled my eyes and just waited for him to break character.

After a while, he relaxed and removed his hand from my mouth. "Apologies. I'm in need of a book."

I wanted to tell him he was in need of some hand soap but didn't fancy my chances in a fight with him. So, I instead asked: "What kind of book?"

"The Prophecy of the Dark King. I assume you have it."

I laughed, "You assume wrong. Very few copies of that book actually exist. You'd be better off going to Skytown to read the prophecy."

"Skytown is too far. I need it now."

"Well, sorry, but I can't help you."

"I'm willing to pay handsomely."

"Good luck. The few collectors who own a copy will never sell it. Trust me, my boss has tried."

"They haven't met me yet, but that doesn't change the facts. I need it soon. I feel something awful is about to happen."

"Well, good luck with that," I told him, "enjoy your LARPing session."

He just glared at me, before huffing and strolling out the door.

Now, of course, me being me, I thought that was the end of it. Another dissatisfied customer. Except, well, it wasn't. Not twenty minutes later, when the sun was already starting to set, someone else showed up. Another cloaked figure dressed up in an even edgier outfit. He kept a black hood over his head, which must have been enchanted because I couldn't even see his face.

"The Dark King's Prophecy," he whispered in a shallow, dissonant voice.

The hairs stood up on the back of my neck, the room seeming to chill at his command. The Glowstone lamps dimmed momentarily, before bouncing back to full power.

"Another one of you LARPers? Look I'm sorry but I told your friend I don't have that book."

A growl emerged from whatever counted for his mouth. The cold winds returned, and I pulled my leather tunic tight around me. The figure briefly scanned the shelves, before sweeping his cape up and leaving the library.

"Come again!" I shouted after him, though I doubted he ever would.

Still, very weird day. Can't say we often get weird people like that in the shop. At least they didn't cause any trouble.

Trouble is just something I'm no good at dealing with.

DAY 5

what just happened

I don't even

will write more tomorrow

need 2 run

DAY 6

I'm safe, diary. That's the most important thing.

Yeah, that's right. I'm safe, I'm safe...

But everything I've ever known is gone.

How do I even begin to explain it? Where the Nether do I start? Just... I don't know. I saw everything happen, from the emergence of that *thing* to my town getting destroyed and and

Okay, time out. I'm gonna try and start from the beginning.

Yesterday. It happened yesterday afternoon.

It was during my lunch break. I'd sat down with a loaf of bread and was enjoying myself in the back of the library. I was about halfway through my meal when I heard a noise upfront. A ringing bell, signifying someone had entered. I found this weird because normally I lock the library during lunchtime. Don't need people stepping in and absconding with my precious literature.

Whatever. So, I went to see what it was, except there was no one there. But the door was moving by itself.

Opening and closing, like it was possessed. So, I locked it and went back to my lunch.

Not two minutes later, it happened again. Opening and closing on its own, even though I'd locked it. Weird, right? Anyway, I locked it again, making sure to have done it exactly right. I didn't even make it back to the backroom before it opened again. Annoyed, I went outside to see if there was anything causing the problem.

And oh brother, you have no idea what I just witnessed.

It was massive. Gargantuan. A behemoth of unparalleled size and scale. It darkened the sky with its very presence and bestowed judgment through a single massive eye encompassing its head. Black was its nature and black its color, it hung in the sky like an all-encompassing shadow. Crowds gathered to witness its coming, whispering theories and fearful thoughts among themselves. The few soldiers garrisoned ordered the people back inside...

And then, it let loose an almighty roar.

It shook the very foundation of the world. Houses crumbled and collapsed beneath it. Panes of glass shattered with an ear-piercing shriek. I could feel it howling into my very soul, and I fell to the ground, struggling to breathe.

After an agonizing amount of time passed, the screeching stopped. The great eye gazed over us as if searching for something...

It wiped out an entire street.

In one epic blast, energy poured from its eye and into the ground below. A bright light encompassed it, leaving nothing in its wake. Buildings, items, and people, all swallowed up. So what else could I do but run?

I fled for the stables. Behind me, I could hear screams and shouts of terror. Explosions rocked the town behind me, the bright light singing shrilly. I didn't look back. I leaped onto the first horse I saw and rode out of town. Barely any items on me. Just the clothes on my back, my diary and a couple of emeralds.

I didn't stop riding until I came upon this inn. By that point, I was exhausted and starving, so I had no choice but to stop. I used the emeralds to get myself a room and meal. Judging from the look on the innkeeper's face, he'd heard what happened but didn't question me about it. For that, I'm grateful.

I've been in my room since I arrived. I just needed to write all of this down, just to understand what happened. To accept it, even. It was so surreal, like nothing I've ever seen before. That creature... no adventurer has ever mentioned encountering something like that. There's been no mention of it in legend or stories or prophecy either.

I don't understand... what was it that destroyed Jebville?

DAY 7

Well, you'll never guess who I ran into.

Do you remember that I mentioned a strange man in black robes visited the library, looking for a certain book? Well, he's here. And not just by coincidence. He asked for me personally, demanding to speak to "the one descended from Silverblade". I tried to slip out as soon as the innkeeper gave him the information, but he caught me before I reached the door.

"Some hero you are," he told me as he shoved me into a corner.

"Excuse me?" I glared at him, "You look more suited for battle than me. How come you didn't take that thing on?"

"I did," he replied glumly, "I was the only one who made it."

"Sorry to hear about your LARPers."

He growled, "We're not LARPers. We're heroes. Protectors of Minecraft and its inhabitants. And we just got crushed. We could have used your help back there."

"Riiight," I sipped from his drink, "what good does a librarian do against a monster like that?"

"I don't need a librarian. I need a Silverblade."

"Good luck finding one."

"You are a Silverblade, yes?"

"In name only. I'm not my father or his descendants."

"Doesn't matter. We need a hero."

"And just like that this conversation is over," I stood up to leave but he blocked my path.

"Nuh-uh. Nope."

He started putting his hands on my face and arms as if he was looking for something.

"Can I help you?" I asked him, trying to pull away.

"Just trying to figure out what kind of hex you're under. Must be a pretty powerful one."

"A hex!?"

"Yup. Clearly, you've been possessed or something. Maybe the Flayer's doing. Or ·mayhap some other sorcerer's work."

"Uh-huh. Tell me, just why do you think I'm under some kind of spell?"

"Because you don't want to help battle the forces of evil! What kind of Silverblade are you?"

He put his hand to my head as if checking my temperature. "How long have they held you hostage? What did they do to you to make you want to work in a library?"

"They didn't do anything!" I finally lost my temper and shoved him away, "How about you stop pestering me and leave me alone!? I'm not the person you think I am. I am not one of the Silverblade heroes, so just get lost and don't bother me again."

He pulled back; his eyes wide at my outburst. He took one final look at me as if to confirm what I just said. With that, he nodded slowly and departed the inn, into the pouring rain once more. I spent the rest of the evening sulking in my corner, trying to get the man out of my thoughts but to no avail. In the end, I just retired to my room to write in my diary.

I don't know what I have to do to convince these people. I'm not a Silverblade. I'm not a hero.

DAY 8

Perhaps I spoke a little bit too soon...

As I write these words, I can see Darkmist in the corner, smugly nodding and smiling at me, like he was right all along. It's taking a lot of effort not to throw this diary straight at him, to wipe that smug look off his face.

Ugh, let me start from the beginning.

It was what looked to be my final day in the inn. I had no more emeralds to pay for my room, so I figured I'd be back on the road by midday. I went outside to check on trusty steed (who I have since decided to name Aaron) and to give him a bucket of water when I heard a shout coming across the road.

I raced over to the scene, where I found a peculiar sight. A young woman clad in grey robes, ax in her hand, stood facing a pair of rough-looking thugs with stone swords. The sun held high above the woman, light sparkling down and giving her a sort of luminescent glow that only added to her extraordinary beaut-

Oh, right, getting off-topic here.

"Yer emeralds or yer life," one of the bandits spat out, along with a couple of his rotten teeth.

"Dun make it hard 'n us," the other grumbled out, his abuse of the English language giving me a strong urge to smack him with a dictionary.

So, I did just that.

Well, it wasn't with a dictionary. I didn't have one. I did happen to have my diary, however. So sorry about that diary. I rushed up behind him and clobbered him with it.

I don't know why I did it.

I just don't know.

One minute I was just watching the confrontation evolve. The next I was standing behind the bandit, dictionary high in the air, as the man screamed at me in fury.

Well, he didn't scream for long. One quick swipe from Greyrobes and the two of them disappeared in a puff of smoke.

"Are... are you okay?" I managed to ask, as Greyrobes brushed herself down.

"Sure was. You kind of stole the spotlight there but whatever."

She walked off towards the inn, not even leaving a thank you. I turned to follow, only to have somebody wrap their arm around my shoulder.

"So," the strange man in black spoke to me, "you're not a hero?"

I growl, "No, I'm not."

"Doesn't look like that from where I'm standing. You saved that girl."

"I did it without thinking!" I protested.

"Oh, I know," he patted me on the head and made his way back to the inn. He paused and turned back to face me one more time.

"And you know what? The best heroes all started out by saving someone without thinking about it."

I was left speechless.

"The name is Darkmist. You can bunk with me"

And so that's how I met Darkmist, one of the most legendary heroes in all of Minecraftia.

DAY 9

Well, it looks like we've got ourselves a little crew now.

Remember Greyrobes? Turns out her name is Lady Grey. How fitting. Almost sounds like the name of a murder mystery character. But she's staying at the inn now, and she's taken quite the interest in myself and Darkmist. I mean, I'm quite the catch so there's no way she wouldn't be enamored by my charm.

Crud, she's looking this way, better pretend I'm writing something clever.

Huh. Don't know why I wrote the word "crew" earlier. These guys aren't my team or anything. I've just agreed to help them with one little thing and that's it. I refuse to be part of some stupid adventuring party. Nuh-uh, not doing it.

My bed at the inn.

Just so you know diary, both Lady Grey and Darkmist are looking for none other than the "Prophecy of the Dark King". That book Darkmist wanted when he visited the library.

"Where did you say it was again?" He'd asked me earlier that evening.

"Skytown. The site of the original prophecy. I have no idea where you'd find a book version, so that's your best bet."

"Well it's a bit too late to prevent the prophecy, but perhaps there's something in there that can help us?"

"Some line about a hero?" Lady Grey offered up as she sharpened her ax.

"Exactly. Something about the destined warrior who shall confront the forces of evil."

I scratched my non-existent beard at this. "I'm sorry, but your plan is to head over to Skytown *hoping* there's something in the prophecy that will help you?"

Darkmist glared at me, "Got any better ideas?"

"Sure do," I announced, "running. Far away from this place. Minecraftia is almost limitless. If we get a head start then that thing won't even find our future generations, let alone us."

"Uh-huh," Darkmist tapped his foot, "see here's the thing. I'm a hero, remember? I'm not about to turn tail and run."

"Well that's your problem," I shrugged before turning to Lady Grey, "what about it? It'll be more than enough adventure without taking on that giant creature."

"No thanks," she replied curtly, "I think I'll go and actually be brave."

Ouch. That cut deep. I didn't open my mouth for a while. I instead listened to Darkmist and Lady Grey, as they debated the best way to get to Skytown. Darkmist suggested Elytras but they figured they'd break before reaching Skytown. Lady Grey proposed a Minecart launched skyward by way of a TNT cannon.

"Come again?" Darkmist blinked.

"TNT canon propulsion. Trust me I've done the maths on this. It'll be fine... Probably."

"Uh-huh. I'm gonna take a hard pass on that one."

And back to the drawing board they went. From an extremely long fishing rod to building a massive dirt tower, the suggestions went back and forth until...

"How about using an airship?" I groaned, finally sick of their stupid ideas.

They both looked at me like I was crazy.

"Airships? When was the last time somebody used an airship?" Lady Grey asked.

"Well, it turns out that the less fortunate of us have different means of transportation. An airship would do us just fine in reaching Skytown."

"I know what they are," she hissed at me, "I learned to fly one. But those things are ancient. Slow and prone to breaking down."

"I can't think of anything else to help us to Skytown," Darkmist admitted. "But we're gonna need a guide to get us to the airstrip."

Lady Grey grinned at me, a smug look in her eyes. I sighed. I had been to the airstrip once before on a business trip. I doubted my abilities to lie, and if I tried to run no doubt Darkmist would tackle me to the ground. There was no getting out of this anytime soon, was there?

"Alright," I moan, "you win. I'll take you to the airstrip. But that's it. Afterward, I want nothing to do with this stupid adventure."

"This *stupid adventure* is about saving the world," said Darkmist, "but that's fine. You'd only be good for soaking up damage anyway."

I kept my mouth shut. No point correcting him on that one. We finalized our plans and decided we'd head off in the morning. Yet whilst Darkmist and Lady Grey drifted off into slumber, I didn't have nearly as much luck. I lay awake tossing and turning, as thoughts of a grizzly end refused to leave my mind.

That's why I've spent the past hour or so writing this entry out. I hate to admit it diary, but I am genuinely scared of what comes next. What if that creature catches up to us? Or worse, what if its friends do? Because I've heard enough Silverblade heroics to know that the bad guy always has his little minions...

And I doubt this creature is different in that regard.

DAY 10

Huh, off to a peaceful enough start so far.

We were met with a blazing sun on the morning of our departure, the clouds sleeking away in their master's presence. Lady Grey procured two more steeds from the nearby town, and the three of us began our journey.

Our ride took us southward, far from the inn and even further from Jebville. We passed small villages with squid-nosed inhabitants. We sauntered down cobbled roads and streets of excellent craftsmanship. We trotted by the crystalline waters of the Dinnerbone River, the surface sparkling like stars beneath a microscope. We tripped and stumbled through thickets of vines and uneven terrain, passing through a rough jungle.

Yet despite all these challenges and tribulations, we persevered. And the wonders we saw. Jeb above, words alone do it an injustice. Jungle trees that crashed into the heavens like great oaken protectors. A city of iron and gold, symbols of craftmanship and riches forged into one. Even the scant creatures that greeted us were a delight. A herd of cows heralded our arrival into farmland. Deeper still, we watched a solitary ocelot drink from a puddle.

I don't remember the last time I saw creatures like these.

Even still, I must remember the mission. Adventuring truly isn't the life for me. Not with the awful food and uncomfortable bedding it offers. No, as soon as I've brought those two to Skytown, I'm done. When the forces of evil are beaten (as they always are, with or without a Silverblade) and Jebville is rebuilt, then I can return to the wonderful life I had before. Stacking shelves in the library.

Sigh. I already miss it.

DAY 11

Something is following us.

In the wee hours of the morning, as I struggled to sleep, Darkmist rose suddenly. Bow drawn, he fired it off into the nearby woods. Two arrows followed in quick succession. Then, a gasp. A horrible, raspy voice. It was like worms with teeth burrowing into your ears. I covered my ears but Darkmist shrugged it off. He fired a fourth time.

The noise stopped.

He approached the tree line slowly, arrow knocked. Lady Grey had stirred by now and followed, ax in hand. The two passed into the woods, where they remained for several minutes. I kept an eye on the camp, shaking in my sleep bag the whole time. I mean, err, watching bravely for any sign of foe that would dare to steal our pork chops.

Eventually, they returned, muttering among themselves.

"... you think *he* serves this creature?" I caught Lady Grey saying.

"Quite possibly. Perhaps he served it from the very beginning. If so, we must be on guard."

"A difficult foe, but easily driven away."

"Yet you need only drop your guard once around him, and your downfall is assured. We'll have to keep watch at night from now on."

"Very well. Shall I take the first watch?"

"No, get some rest. No way I'm sleeping for a while."

"As you wish."

Lady Grey retreated to her tent. Darkmist took a seat on a stump of wood. He placed his bow and a single arrow into his lap. His eyes returned to the woods, where he watched. Silence descended onto the camp for a few minutes more, until I found myself with the urge to speak.

"Err, hello."

"Hey."

"Are you alright on your own?"

"Yeah," Darkmist affirmed, "I'll be fine. Not the first time I've had to keep watch."

"Alright," I nodded. "Um, but if you get tired, feel free to let me know."

Darkmist sighed, "You don't have to *pretend* to care about this, Axel. Just get us to our destination, that's all we want from you."

Shame burned in my gut as I turned away from Darkmist. I tried to get some sleep, but I just found myself tossing and turning all night long, his words ringing out in my head. Pretending? I wasn't pretending. I genuinely wanted to help. I might as well, considering I'm being dragged along for this ride.

Well, whatever, if he wants to stay up all night without any relief or company, then that's his problem.

DAY 12

Alright, I think we're safe.

I actually managed to get some sleep last night. When I woke, I found Darkmist in the same position I'd left him in. Sitting on the stump, staring straight ahead. He gave me a grunt of acknowledgment as I rose from my slumber.

"Morning," I relit the campfire with some flint and steel, "do you want some coffee?"

"Please," he rasped with a tired voice. Guess he *wasn't* used to staying up late.

I brewed him a bowl which he slurped down eagerly.

"Thanks," he said, a bit of energy back in his voice.

Lady Grey was quick to rise soon afterward, and we enjoyed a relatively okay breakfast of apples and bread. Not my first choice but I was hungry so no complaints.

"So," I struck up a bit of courage once we got back on the road, "can you tell me about what happened last night? Why you guys were so spooked?"

Darkmist didn't reply at first. Lady Grey pretended she didn't hear, instead riding on ahead to "scout things out". Darkmist gently tapped the reins of his saddle, and I assumed he was mulling things over in his head.

"The Flayer."

"Come again?" I asked. Wasn't familiar with this mob.

"A servant of the Ender King. Supposedly he was once a great and mighty warrior who stormed the End with fire and fury."

"The Ender King?" I raised an eyebrow, "You mean the Ender Dragon? That thing has been dead for years."

"No, I mean the Ender King. The true ruler of that realm, and the creature that's currently destroying Minecraft."

Oh... oh no.

"The Ender King created the End and the Ender Dragons."

"Ender Dragons? As in plural?"

Darkmist nodded, "Yeah. Your dad wasn't the only one to beat one, even though he was the first. We found out the hard way that the End wasn't safe when we returned for an expedition. There were dozens of the things flying around. We did manage to beat them, eventually, but we lost a lot of good people."

He sighed, "No Ender King though. Although we'd heard rumors about him in the past, and even discovered information about him in some ancient scrolls, we figured he was just a relic of the old eras of Minecraft. Something that had existed once, but no longer."

"Well, he's back now," I so intelligently pointed out.

"That he is, but back to the topic at hand. The Flayer is supposedly a servant of the Ender King that lives among us. A dark shape wielding the power of the dark, cloaked in darkness and spreading darkness wherever he... well, you get the point."

I thought about it for a moment, "Does he happen to wear lots of dark robes, with a hood that doesn't show his face?"

Darkmist pulled his steed to a stop, "You met him!?"

"I think. He came to my library just after you left."

Darkmist thought about this, "Makes sense. I thought I felt his presence in the area. What did he want?"

"Same thing as you. The Prophecy of the Dark King."

Darkmist swore under his breath, "That's not good. He's probably looking to destroy it before we get our hands on it. You didn't tell him about Skytown, did you?"

I shook my head, "No I didn't."

"Alright, that's good. The less he knows, the better. Still, if The Flayer is looking for it then that makes me think we're on the right track. There must be something we can use in there."

We rode onwards, aiming to catch up to Lady Grey.

"Say, I never asked but... did you guys think the Ender King was going to show up? All of the heroes were gathered in the town, right?"

"Most of them," Darkmist nodded, "and yeah, we figured something was up. One of them, Seer, can peek into the future. She reckoned to have seen something about Jebville getting destroyed. So we all went there, figuring we could stop it."

The lone hero silently looked off into the sky.

DAY 13

Things are still okay.

After that conversation I had with Darkmist, I managed to piece together what had happened. Most of the heroes that went to Jebville? They're not with us anymore. We haven't seen the Ender King since our encounter at Jebville, but if he's still destroying towns and cities then there's barely anyone to defend Minecraftia.

Ugh, how did I get wrapped into this? Why am I carrying this stupid guilty feeling in my gut, wherever I go? None of this is my fault, and I never wanted anything to do with it to begin with. I'm just gonna get them to the airstrip and that's that. They'll get to Skytown, figure out the prophecy and save the world. Me? I'm gonna relax on a beach somewhere until the world is safe and sound.

Later...

So, I got the chance to have a proper conversation with Lady Grey.

We stopped off in an inn for the night, finally finding a place to stay that wasn't under some stupid trees or on hard ground. I was just getting ready to sleep when I found that ax-wielder outside, staring into the night sky.

"Hey," she said as I approached.

"Hi," I replied in kind.

And that was the entirety of our conversation for a good ten minutes. Still, the silence wasn't awkward or anything. It was nice, just enjoying the peaceful night sky, the shining stars and the occasional firework as some lunatic across the street decided he was going to celebrate Christmas about five months early.

"Sorry about before."

"Hm?"

If I hadn't seen her lips move, I would have sworn I misheard her.

"About my attitude. Honestly? I expected you to turn tail and flee the moment things got tough. But you've stuck by us so far, helping us out where you can. So thanks. A lot of people are gonna owe you a huge debt when this is over."

"If they remember me," I joked, "don't think the guide will be remembered as much as the heroes who saved the day."

"We'll see," she winked at me.

After a brief moment, a question popped into my mind.

"Sooo," I began, "why'd you decide to come with us? To get wrapped in all of this?"

She scratched her head, "Revenge I guess."

And before I could question her further, she just walked back inside. She's a strange character, Lady Grey. I don't even know her first name. In fact, I don't even know Darkmist's name. Is that the whole "protecting his secret identity thing?"

Guess I'll have to find out later.

DAY 14

HOLY NETHER!

What... what just happened!?

I'm still trying to make sense of it all... there's no way I actually did that? Right?

Buckle up diary, this is one heck of a ride.

It happened around noon. We'd left the inn and continued our journey. Based on my calculations, we were only a day or so away from Airstrip Delta. The last place in Minecraftia we'd be able to get a ride to Skytown. Wanting to get there by nightfall, Darkmist set a horrifically grueling pace that left us exhausted. We had no choice but to rest up at lunchtime.

"Pair of pansies," Darkmist shook his head as Lady Grey and I flopped to the ground, totally beat. "Alright, take a ten-minute break."

Darkmist paced the clearing where we stopped. A small opening in a forest of pine. The ground was uneven and trampled, clearly a route taken by dozens of people before. Above us, a few birds soared and fluttered among the trees, cheerily chirping away...

And then a dark shadow set itself upon the ground, and we sprang to our feet.

Darkmist drew his bow, whilst Lady Grey moved to back him up with her ax. I elected to seize a stick I had lying in my inventory. The three of us shuffled to the center of the clearing, covering all directions. There was no need for words. Even though I'd never seen this creature before, a shadow doesn't arrive without reason.

"The Flayer," Darkmist confirmed my suspicions, "be ready."

The horses trotted around anxiously. I extended a hand and gently stroked Aaron's mane, trying to calm him. He shivered but softened under my touch and remained in place. A chilling wind blasted into the clearing, shaking me to my bones. My gut froze up, and my teeth chattered away. Was this merely the cold? Or pure fear?

Then, a hissing. A low, terrible sound that snuck its way into my head. My head flooded with thoughts. Memories from my childhood, recollections from last week and vivid images of the destruction left by the Ender King. Joining this dissonance was a chorus of terror and bleakness. Whispers of *failure* and *pathetic* and *disappointment*.

It took all of my composure to stay standing. I looked at my friends, who were just about holding on themselves. Darkmist with his teeth gritted and Lady Grey with her eyes shut, mumbling under her breath.

And then came the Flayer.

He swooped down from the trees, slicing at us with a great black scythe. Darkmist and Lady Grey dived out of the way, whilst I fell to the ground. The scythe slashed over me, barely missing me as I dropped to the ground. The Flayer rose his scythe, planting it into the ground next to my head. I rolled out of reach. Once. Twice. Three times he struck, with me barely able to avoid it.

"SUFFER!" It hissed, only to be tackled into a tree.

Darkmist, having shoved the Flayer away, drew his sword. Blade and scythe met, sounding a greeting with a teeth-scraping clang. Darkmist struck twice more. The Flayer parried, slicing away. Darkmist slashed low but the Flayer knocked it aside effortlessly, swinging his own weapon towards Darkmist's exposed neck. He ducked under it, closing the distance between the two and plunging his weapon forward.

I'm... not sure what happened. One moment the Flayer was there, and next, he vanished in a puff of smoke. Darkmist almost fell forward, only to be caught by the Flayer, now reappeared behind him. Darkmist turned, and the Flayer placed its tentacle-like arm upon Darkmist's forehead.

"You will serve."

"I... will serve." Darkmist mirrored.

Darkmist turned to face us, his eyes a vibrant purple.

Yeah, this situation was looking a tad awful.

I've read enough books to know how this goes down. I didn't give Darkmist the chance to strike first, knowing full well he was about to attack us. So I threw a bucket at him. I know, didn't exactly have a weapon on me so I made do with what I had. It clanged against his head, and for the briefest moment, I thought I saw his eyes return to their regular shade of blue. Didn't last long. He shook the pain off and ran towards me, bringing his sword down.

Only to be met with Lady Grey's ax.

"Alright Axel, hit him!" Lady Grey ordered.

"I've got a better idea," I replied, grabbing the bucket again. "I'll stick him with this!"

I ran forward and tried to ram the bucket down on his head. Instead, he sidestepped, allowing Lady Grey to fall forward. Right into the trajectory of my bucket, the iron crown fitting snuggly on her head.

"AXEL YOU IDIOT!" Lady Grey echoed as she stumbled around the campsite, tripping over herself.

Oops.

Darkmist looked over to Lady Grey, then back at me. He shrugged, a tight grin forming on his face. He stomped over to me, raising his sword high in the air. I leaped to the side once more. My eyes scoured the campsite, looking for something I could use. Anything!

Under one of the trees, the Flayer watched with an intense glare. Almost like he was enjoying the spectacle.

I finally found my savior in the form of a fallen wood block. I rose it high above my head as Darkmist struck.

The blade lodged itself in the wood, and he yanked it free. He slashed from left to right. I parried with my tree. He laughed and smote the wood a final time, hewing it into nothing. I was defenseless.

For a moment, I thought this was it. The end...

At least it was until Lady Grey smacked Darkmist with the bucket.

CLANG! Darkmist stumbled, clutching his (probably) aching skull. Woozy, he swayed from left to right, the purple in his eyes fading away.

"Awuh?" He asked Lady Grey.

Lady Grey smacked him again, knocking him out for good.

"COME ON!" She yelled, throwing Darkmist over her shoulder.

The Flayer screamed. A piercing wail that shook the trees and rattled my brains. Lady Grey tossed the bucket at it, and he barely sidestepped it. He watched with angered eyes as we leaped onto our steeds, abandoning most of our supplies as we fled towards Airstrip Delta.

Goosebumps perked up across my body, the hairs standing on the back of my neck. I knew he was watching me.

DAY 15

Okay, so I should probably explain the situation.

Good news is we escaped the Flayer. One of Lady Grey's agents (yes, apparently she has those) sent a message saying he'd been spotted in Chirpatown. The opposite direction to where we're headed. If he's looking for us then he's looking in the wrong place. This means the path to Skytown should be free. Speaking of which, we've also arrived at Airstrip Delta. We're staying at a healer's lodge whilst we wait for Darkmist to recover.

Airstrip Delta.

Now for the bad news.

Airstrip Delta is currently locked down. Thousands of Minecraftians have gathered here to board airships to other parts of the realm, but the fact is there just isn't enough airships. The flights are being processed slowly, to the point where there are several days of waiting. Every day we spend here is a day the Flayer or the Ender King can reach Skytown before us.

Us...

I've been thinking more and more about that as well. About how I didn't want to go on this stupid adventure, how I was just going to be the guide. I didn't mention it before, but when I was fighting with Darkmist there was... something inside of me. This burning sensation, but not at all unpleasant. This fire, that yearned to be stoked.

Is it my lineage calling me? The voices of Silverblades past, telling me to pick up my mantle? To become the hero I'm supposedly destined to be? To fight the forces of darkness and save the world from certain doom?

I don't know. I really don't know anymore.

Later...

Darkmist is up again.

He seemed a little confused and disorientated, but a healing potion took care of that. And once he heard that he'd been knocked out by Lady Grey with a bucket, he laughed until it hurt.

"Quite the fighter," he complimented her, "and the same goes for you, Axel."

"Me?"

"Yeah. Not many people can go up against Minecraft's third strongest hero."

"I thought you dropped down in the rankings?" Lady Grey pointed out.

"Fine, fourth-strongest hero."

"I heard it was fifth," I added sheepishly.

"Ugh, sure, beat on the guy who's suffering from a concussion." Darkmist rubbed his head. "So what's the situation?"

We filled him in on what was happening in Chirpatown but he didn't seem that fussed by any of it. "Doesn't sound like that big of a problem to me. We just need to think creatively."

"Couldn't you requisition one of the vessels?" I asked him, "Considering you're a hero of Minecraft."

Darkmist seemed to bristle at that, "Um, about that."

"He's got a criminal record," Lady Grey chimed in.

That was news to me, "Say what?"

Darkmist sighed, "I wasn't always a hero. At one point I did happen to work with a group of griefers. I was one of the most notorious criminals in Minecraft."

I blinked, "You can't be serious."

"'fraid so. I was one of the worst until I ran into none other than Shade Silverblade."

"My great grandfather!?" No, this didn't make any sense. Shade Silverblade's epic battle against the Rowdy Boyz took place about a hundred years ago. There was no way that Darkmist had been present for it.

"How old do you think I am?"

"Eh... forty?" I attempted to guess.

"Two-hundred and eighty-six."

My jaw dropped, "What on earth?"

"Long story," Darkmist grinned, "but let's just say that Shade Silverblade didn't seal all of my abilities away. I managed to keep a few of them."

"Including immortality?"

"You know it," Darkmist nodded, "I will live forever. As long as I don't get stabbed or shot with an arrow. But things like aging, sickness and even my mother's cooking won't put an end to my life."

"That's incredible." I managed to sputter out, "But you're telling me your criminal record won't let you acquire a ship?"

"Nope. Although I am a Hero of Minecraftia, I'm still technically in a probation period. I don't get all of the same perks as most people my rank do. I need to earn them."

"And how long have you been a hero?"

"Oh, roundabout thirty years now."

"Great."

"This isn't helping," Lady Grey shook her head, "so we need a new plan. What the heck are we supposed to do if we can't requisition a vessel?"

We thought about it for a few moments, wrapping our head on just how we were supposed to get past the crowds and on our way to Skytown. Until finally, a particularly devious thought popped into my mind. One I'd never look to share normally, but right now we were lacking in more moral options.

"We could steal it."

DAY 16

Hey, diary! Haven't had much of a chance to talk these past few hours. Lemme fill you in on the details.

So after I proposed that little idea, things were a little silent around here. Despite that though, Darkmist and Lady Grey quickly warmed up to it. Mentions of "the greater good" and "I wasn't nearly wild enough in my teenage years so let's do it".

Still struggling to accept the fact that Darkmist used to be some criminal. I mean, he totally has the look for it and I always got this strange vibe from him that he wasn't exactly who he said he was. Even so, I didn't expect it to be... this. A former griefer who fought against my great-grandfather. Still, if he's on our side now that makes him a formidable ally.

Huh. I just had a thought. I wonder how well Shade sealed Darkmist's abilities away. I mean, I'm not saying we *should* unleash them but if we could, imagine the firepower we'd have on our side. Heck, it might be the means to defeat the Ender King.

Oh, look at me, thinking like some hero. I'm still thinking about it y'know. Still not sure what to make of this life of adventure and... and...

Okay, I'm ranting. Back to the situation at hand.

We're planning to steal the airship in a few days. Right now it just isn't possible with all the new arrivals at Airstrip Delta and the number of guards they have stationed. Darkmist reported that there's a window of time where we can steal an airship when it arrives at the Airstrip. Y'see when they arrive, they're loosely guarded and easy to swipe, and the next one to arrive is in two days.

That's the easy part.

There's a couple of other hiccups in the plan. For one, we can't just steal an airship. Minecrafters have had this problem of airship theft many times in the past, so they created a solution. The Redstone Authentication System (or RAS for short). This tricky little system prevents people from stealing airships. The pilots are given a Redstone keycard which they need to power on the vessel. Tricky, but doable. And Lady Grey reckons she can hack the system if we can't get the keycard.

Still, there's one other thing we can't get around. It's also one of the reasons why Airstrip Delta is seeing so many refugees showing up. Apparently, the Ender King has released some kind of monsters. Flying beasts that burn anything they spot. Ender Wyverns. Kinda like smaller versions of the Ender Dragon. Not as powerful of course, but still nasty opponents to be fighting. In order to fight against them, Airstrip Delta has begun creating maps detailing their locations and flight patterns. We're going to need a steal a copy of this map just before leaving, else the Ender Wyverns might just shoot us down.

Oh, and did I mention security? Diamond-armored soldiers with enchanted blades and bows. Even a couple of automated dispensers. And according to Lady Grey, if we don't steal the vessel quickly then the guards will just destroy the engines and stop us from leaving.

So yeah, this is really gonna be a tough one. Even for a former griefer, a librarian and a Lady Grey.

Speaking of which, Darkmist wants us to do team-building exercises.

I know, I'm as surprised as you are. I thought I was a perfectly good partner to work with, but apparently not.

We've been doing exercises just behind the inn. From running an obstacle course with our limbs tied together to exchanging honest compliments.

It hasn't been going very well. I said Lady Grey reminded me of Squidword, the noblest and fairest of all the villagers in Minecraftia. Darkmist barely managed to pull her off me, as she screamed about me "calling her big-nosed". I'm not quite sure what she's on about.

So yeah, that's the situation. A difficult heist to pull off, the Ender King growing in power with each passing day AND a team which can barely work together.

Overall, I rate our chances 50/50.

DAY 17

Trouble on the roads.

Apparently, the Flayer didn't take too kindly to the fact we managed to evade him. When he discovered we weren't in Chirpatown, he burnt it to the ground. Since then he's been prowling the roads north of here, accosting travelers and transforming them into his thralls. Already the guards have had to fight off some of the Flayer's thralls. They tried to enter the city but were swiftly pushed back.

The city is fine, which is great. But the fact that they used to be people is what really twists in my gut. Darkmist informed them of the method we discovered to free them from the Flayer's control, but the guards don't want to try it. Too dangerous, they say. And they're not wrong. If they screw up then the whole city and airstrip will fall.

Which doesn't make it any better.

These are people that are suffering. I shouldn't give a darn because I'm not supposed to be a hero. I was destined to be a librarian. But even so, every time I think about them there's this twisting feeling in my gut.

A horrible, burning sensation that seems to scream at me. Wills me to march outside the city and find these thralls to save them.

One of the villages attacked by the Flayer.

Then common sense takes over before I'm halfway out the door.

I... I don't know what to do with myself anymore.

Later...

Lady Grey has some news on the airship.

Apparently, there's a small cargo vessel arriving very soon. To top it off, some of the guards got injured in the attack from the thralls. Lady Grey also thinks she can get one of her agents to temporarily shut down the

Redstone power plant, to switch off the dispensers. If so, we've got this in the bag. There will be almost nothing stopping us from getting to Skytown.

Honestly? I don't think we're gonna get a better shot at this. Darkmist and Lady Grey are both incredibly hyped...

So why do I feel so awful?

DAY 18

Things have gone from bad to worse.

The good news is that the airship is going to arrive tonight. That gives us our window to escape out of here and make it to Skytown. We've been rehearsing the plan and it's actually going really well. We might actually manage to pull things off. Heck, I can even swing a sword now! Life is going great.

Here's the bad news: the Ender King is on his way here.

Lady Grey's spy network confirmed it. Something is drawing it towards Airstrip Delta. We're not sure what, but there's no mistaking it's making its way here. Maybe the Flayer has summoned it, or maybe there's something it wants here. Either way, we can't afford to stick around...

Except, I'm wondering more and more if we should stick around, if only for a bit longer. Because people are being seized at an alarming frequency. The villages around Airstrip Delta have been targeted by the Flayer and the inhabitants have been turned into thralls. The Flayed, they're being called. The survivors have come to Airstrip Delta, traumatized by the events that have happened. They're devastated about the people they've lost, and they're looking for someone to help them.

I talked it over with Darkmist last night. It didn't go well.

"I'm sorry," he told me whilst patting my head, "but that's not something we can do."

"But you're a hero!" I argued, "It's your job to help people."

"Aye, it is. To help as many people as I can. Delaying the plan to save a few people seized by the Flayer isn't going to do us much good. They'll be fine in the short-term, but if us delaying the plan results in the Ender King winning, then we're done for. The people we saved won't stay saved for very long."

"I'm with Darkmist on this," Lady Grey flicked her white hair, "I don't like it any more than you do Axel, but if we make it to Skytown and find a way to defeat the Ender King then we can find a way to free them. They'll just have to put up with it for a bit longer."

"Put up with it!?" I stamped my foot, "These are innocent lives who are suffering, and you're willing to just push them aside? What if we're wrong about Skytown? What if this adventure is for nothing?"

"Then we lose," Darkmist shrugged, "and then nothing matters."

I glared at him, "Tell me something. How did it feel to be trapped under the sway of the Flayer?"

He hesitated at that. He turned to leave the room but I grabbed his arm to stop him.

"Tell me, Darkmist."

He sighed, "For a librarian, you're too darned stubborn. Alright, fine. It was horrible. One of the worst experiences of my life. I was totally awake throughout it, unable to do anything. A passenger in my own body whilst the Flayer took it for a joyride, pouring fire into my very veins. I never want to go through something like that again."

For a moment, I thought I'd managed to get through to him.

"And that's why we need to steal that airship tonight. To stop the Flayer from continuing this."

"No!" I yelled at him, "We have to save those people tonight!"

"We can't risk the mission," Lady Grey chimed in. "Going against the Flayer is a dangerous game. We could be injured, or worse. Then we're well and truly stuck."

"She's right. I'm right. Get some sleep Axel, and leave the tough decisions to the heroes. Your work here is done, so go home."

The smug idiots both left the room after that, and I was fuming. Abandoning innocent people to their fate? This was ridiculous! We're heroes, are we not?

I... I'm a hero too.

I know I am. I might not have wanted this, but this is the position I'm in now. The task I have been given, to save this world from the Ender King, is something I'll carry out. It might be scary, I might want to turn tail and run, but I can't give up now. And I certainly can't abandon innocent people behind. And with that said...

Tonight, I'm going after them.

It's quite possible I won't be coming back. Quite probable, in fact. I won't have Darkmist's battle-hardened experience or Lady Grey's powerful ax arm to back me up. It'll just be me, my wits and all the stories I read while I was bored in a library.

It'll be enough. I hope.

Wish me luck diary. This might be the last time we speak. If so, it's been a real pleasure to document my adventure within...

DAY 19

As you can probably gather by the fact I am writing, I'm alive!

I made it diary! I made it back! I'm okay! I proved Darkmist and Lady Grey wrong! I did it! I did it! The people are safe!

Okay, I should probably start from the beginning on this one. Buckle up, because this adventure is absolutely amazing and one I'm gonna be telling my friends for decades to come. Heck, I might even write a book about it when this whole thing is over. But I'm just blabbering on now, so let's get to the real meat of things.

Just how did I save the Flayed from the Flayer?

Well, first of all, I needed to figure out where the thralls were being kept. So that evening, I snuck out to one of the few villages in the area which hadn't yet been visited by the Flayer. I set myself up on a towering hill, crafted myself a little telescope and just waited for things to happen...

Watching the Flayer show up, break into houses and brainwash the people living inside... it wasn't easy. That burning feeling in my gut? It kept flaring up. Kept pushing me onward, demanding that I head down there and do something to save those people. I had to keep refusing it, telling it that I would help. Eventually. Surprisingly the burning desire for justice doesn't want to listen to logic.

At any rate, I managed to hold myself in place until the Flayer was done with the village. He must have enslaved at least twenty people. Those who were left were cold, frightened and miserable. Yet once the Flayer departed, I made my way into the village.

"I need all your buckets," I announced to their confused faces, "don't worry, I'm a hero."

After some convincing, during which I had to reassure them I'd be bringing their friends and family back, I was gifted not only the buckets but also some armor and even a nice iron blade. It was a little worn and hummed with some faint power, and I was happy to take it. Better that than beating my foes over the head with my diary. I told all the villagers to head for Airstrip Delta, where they would be safe.

With my items gathered, I stopped off at the village well and filled all the buckets. With everything in place, I began following the tracks left in the Flayer's wake. A conga line of footsteps that extended far away from Airstrip Delta, taking me to an old abandoned mine. It was here the resources for Airstrip Delta were gathered and used to build the city/base. After construction was finished, they had no more need for the mine and instead closed it off. It remained abandoned ever since.

The old mine shaft...

At least until now.

A few scant torches lit the entryway to the mine. It was a torrid affair. Formed out of old wood planks and cobweb-tainted fencing. The inside was like the gaping maw of a titan, bleak and lightless, seemingly going on forever. Yet what interested me was the gathering of people outside the mine. At least a hundred, but maybe more. Gathered in a series of circles orbiting the Flayer and his newest victims. For now, he hadn't spotted me.

I should probably preface that at that point, I had no idea if my plan was going to work. I hadn't tested it, and it was only based on pure theory.

I already knew one way of freeing someone from the Flayer was to smack them very hard with a bucket. The trouble was that wasn't possible for the current situation. There were just too many people for me to hit, and it wouldn't take long for them to apprehend me. The Flayer could then turn me into a thrall as well, and it would be mission over. So I needed a different solution.

I was going to soak them all with ice-cold water.

I imagine some of you are probably shaking their heads at my seeming stupidity. Some of you probably wish you could reach through the pages to strangle me. And I get all of that, but just hear me out for a second. I figured that if hitting them in the head with a bucket was good enough, then a similar shock would be enough to break them out of it.

That and something Darkmist said struck me. He mentioned, "pouring fire through his veins" when he was under the influence of the Flayer. So of course, being the genius that I am, I decided that the best thing to counteract fire was water!

Genius, right? Right!?

Yeah okay, I was pretty skeptical myself. But I figured "in for an iron ingot, in for a gold ingot". And so I let loose powerful waves of water that crashed down on the spectators. They shuddered and cried out, falling to the ground like dominos.

Immediately, the Flayer let loose his piercing shriek as the water brushed against him. He vanished in a puff of smoke, reappearing a short distance away. His purple eyes glowed from beneath his hood, as he surveyed the scene and looked for the person responsible. His eyes met with mine and a cold chill seeped into my bones. I shivered and shook, but the Flayer didn't move shift from his spot.

The whispers returned. That chorus of abandonment and loathing, discording right into my soul. I tasted metal and my knees buckled from under me, as the words screamed inside my head. Things like *failure* and *loser*, backed by a bass of low laughter that took such delight in seeing me suffer. I struggled to hold back the tears, to remain composed, anything to break free of this awful prison...

Then, it stopped.

Not slowly fading away, like the sound of a Minecart driving off into the distance, but instead cut off abruptly. I returned to my senses, finding myself laid back on the grass. I jumped to feet, just in time to see the Flayer disappear in a puff of smoke, an arrow protruding from his back. From my blurred vision, I watched as two figures arrived. A man dressed in black robes and a woman with long white hair and the face of an angel.

Darkmist and Lady Grey. A smile warmed my cheeks and I raced over to them with open arms.

Lady Grey promptly planted her fist in my stomach, and I doubled over.

"ARE YOU STUPID!?" She yelled at me, kicking me as she did. "WHAT PART OF FOLLOW THE PLAN DON'T YOU UNDERSTAND!?"

"Owwwww," I groaned.

Darkmist stepped in and gently pulled Lady Grey away, "Come on, he's suffered enough. We'll pummel him later."

Darkmist helped me to my feet, "But that doesn't change the facts. You endangered the mission."

"Wait... you mean the airship?"

"It's gone. Took off a few minutes ago."

The window of opportunity was gone. I opened my mouth to speak but Darkmist shook his head. Lady Grey rounded up the rescued civilians, who were cold, frightened and soaking wet. Together, we made the long march back to Airstrip Delta.

I'll be honest, I wasn't sure what to make of things. I figured Darkmist and Lady Grey were going to dump me off as soon as they made it back to the city. Yet as we walked, a thought did wriggle its way into my head.

"What happened to saving the most amount of people, rather than individuals?"

Darkmist scoffed at me, though I thought I caught the briefest glimpse of a smile on his lips. Lady Grey maintained her angry composure all throughout the trip, even towards the people I'd managed to save. She shot burning looks at me whenever she thought I wasn't looking. Was it perhaps an angry attraction of some kind? Or just straight-up anger?

Not sure, need to figure that one out.

About an hour later, and we found ourselves outside the gates of Airstrip Delta. The guards on duty took a careful look at those present, recognizing a few of the thralls from last time. However, after I explained the situation to him, he told me to wait. He went off for a few minutes, before opening the gates for us.

And inside was such a glorious sight.

Crowds of people had gathered. Citizens of Airstrip Delta of course, but also everybody from the surrounding villages. Mothers and daughters, fathers and sons, and broken up families. Almost everyone present had lost someone to the grasp of the Flayer, but now that person had been brought home.

The two groups met and exchanged hugs, kisses, laughter, and tears. It was a truly beautiful scene, watching this reunification. More than once, a few of the people I saved approached me and offered their thanks and whatever meager possessions they owned. Not gonna lie, some of the shiny stuff there were offering looked pretty nice, but I had to turn them down. Though I did accept an interesting book from one of them.

Throughout Darkmist and Lady Grey watched with apt attention, never speaking nor moving. It was only when the guards transported the crowds elsewhere that they finally approached me to speak with me.

"We... um..." Lady Grey began, scratching her arm. "I just wanted to say that... well, you know..."

Now diary. I am quite a humble person. However, in this situation, I couldn't help but turn things against Lady Grey.

"No, I don't know," I chuckled, "mind telling me?"

"UGH!" She stomped her foot, "You're the worst! I was wrong, okay?"

"Me too," Darkmist chimed in, "and I wanted to thank you."

"Eh?" I raised an eyebrow, "Thank me for what? Doing your job for you?"

"Basically," he nodded, "it is the duty of a hero to protect the innocents, wherever they might be. To guard and protect the realm and its inhabitants, no matter how few they might be. I was ready to forsake that vow, but you kept it for me. So thank you."

"Soooo," I began, "does that make me a hero or-?"

"Absolutely not," Darkmist shut me down, "that was one of the worst rescues I've ever seen. If we hadn't bothered to show up when we did, you'd be in the Flayer's grasp. Points for trying, but we really need to work on your skills."

"Fair enough," I scratched my neck, "so what now?"

"Now, we rest. Tomorrow, we'll pay a visit to the Mayor of Airstrip Delta. I figure that saving a bunch of people from the Flayer should give us all the leverage we need to negotiate an airship out of him."

Phew, my hand is cramping after all of that. Heck, I should really be asleep right now. Busy day tomorrow and all that. But there was one other thing I wanted to mention. That feeling in my gut? The burning feeling that screamed at me to save those people in the first place? It's died right down. It's almost welcoming now, a gentle glow to reassure me I did the right thing.

Guess I might just be a hero after all.

DAY 20

I take it back. Being a hero is a real pain.

We paid a visit to Mayor McBlockers today, the Mayor of Airstrip Delta. As Darkmist mentioned before, he believed he could get permission to use an airship from him. Lady Grey didn't seem convinced so she left the negotiations to us whilst she went to gather some supplies for us. Thinking back, I wish I'd gone with her.

We had an appointment with Mayor McBlockers at about midday. We seated ourselves in his waiting room, a mix between lushness and cheapness. For instance, the secretary's desk? Beautiful and expensive. The seats we were left waiting on? Horrible, hard and rough on the back. Darkmist tried to play it cool by saying he'd slept on worse, though after a few minutes he looked like he was about to start weeping.

Then, of course, the Mayor was late. Oh, his secretary had told us how happy he'd be to see us and that he'd opened his schedule to "meet the legendary Darkmiss and Axer". We didn't bother correcting her but figured the Mayor must want to see us after our deeds the other night. Nope. Kept us waiting an hour before he bothered to show.

When he finally did, allowing us into his office, he prefaced by saying he only a few minutes to "discuss trivial matters."

"Ah yes, trivial matters," Darkmist nodded, "like the very fate of the world?"

He perked up a little bit after this, "Alright you've made your point. Now, what do you want?"

"An airship. We need to borrow one to get us to Skytown."

"Yeah, not happening," the mayor shook his head.

Darkmist glared, "Might I ask why?"

"Too risky, too expensive and right now, we need all the airships we can get, especially if the Ender King is on his way."

"If we don't get an airship, we can't get to Skytown. I'm assuming you know what's in Skytown?"

The mayor nodded slowly, "Yeah, an ancient prophecy that was written a million darn years ago. What about it? You really think it'll have something to stop the Ender King?"

"Maybe," Darkmist shrugged, "better than any other ideas I've heard so far."

"Uh-huh, well no. We're not risking it."

"Can't you contact Skytown?" I offered, "If you won't give us an airship then get them to send the prophecy to us."

"I'm afraid I can't," the mayor shook his head, "communication systems are down right now. And even then, the prophecy's enchantment won't let information leak out like that."

"Huh? What do you mean?"

The mayor sighed, "I don't have time to get history lessons. Now if you have no other business here, please leave me to my work."

Darkmist stood to his feet, slowly. "I'd suggest reconsidering your offer. You could cost the lives of everyone in Airstrip Delta with your short-sightedness."

The mayor glared, "I won't be threatened by some former criminal such as yourself. Now, how about get out of my office before I call security?"

Darkmist laughed, "As if they could stop me, but whatever. Enjoy your day Blockers. Don't come crying to me when you need help."

We left the office before the Mayor could make good on his threat. Outside on the cobble streets, Darkmist looked like he was about to punch the nearest lamppost.

"Great, we did the city a favor and they still won't play ball with us."

"Maybe we can find a pilot who'd be willing to risk taking us?" I offered.

Darkmist thought about it but then shook his head. "Not worth it. Blockers will probably inform all of the pilots about us now, so we can't go down that route. Nope, we're gonna have to go back to Plan A. Steal the airship and make our dramatic escape to Skytown."

I thought about it, "Blockers will probably extend security around the airstrip, y'know."

"Yup, without a doubt. He doesn't trust us."

"So the plan just got even harder?"

"It did."

I shrugged, "Oh well. We'll find a way to pull it off."

"Darn right we will."

Later...

We met with Lady Grey and told her about our meeting. She just laughed it off, stating that stealing an airship was much more fun.

We carefully discussed and rehearsed the plan, deciding to nab an airship tomorrow. Any longer and Blockers might try to move against us some other way. Besides, the Ender King would be here at any moment, so we couldn't afford to hang about.

Darkmist went back into the city that evening. He said he was going to talk with the town guard to make sure the citizens would be okay for when the Ender King arrived. That just left me and Lady Grey. Alone. Which flared my nerves up. Did Darkmist really want to leave me alone with the girl who kicked the snot out of me just the other night?

"Hey," she said.

"HEY!" I accidentally screamed out loud, terror drenching my words. I clasped my mouth shut with my hands, but she just laughed.

"Yeah, I getcha. Sorry about pummeling you the other night."

"Oh, that," I faked a laugh, "it's all good."

She blinked at me, "I mean, erm, if you say so."

A silence settled, and not the peaceful kind. An awkward silence full of coughing and wistful glances at each other. Seconds passed, perhaps even minutes, before it was finally shattered by one of my more intelligent sayings.

"Lovely weather we're having."

"... Yes." She nodded slowly.

IT WAS RAINING OUTSIDE! OH SWEET MERCY, WHAT WAS WRONG WITH ME!?

"Um," I struggled for something to say, "maybe I can ask you a question?"

"I mean, that's a question, but go for it."

"Why'd you join up with us?" I asked.

She hesitated for a moment, gently rubbing her arm. "Umm, that's a good question actually. Maybe because I just want the fame and fortune that comes out of saving the world?"

"Come on," I prodded a little, "it's gotta be something more than that."

"Well... the Ender King blew up my family's factory."

"Family factory... wait a minute!"

I bolted upright, "You're not Lady Grey of Grey Enterprises, are you?"

She giggled, "Oh come on, you don't still think my actual name is Lady Grey, do you? I told you that as a joke."

Oh. Oops. I turned a deep red and her laughter only grew more vocal. She slapped her thigh as tears of joy ran down her face.

"Sorry," she managed to wheeze out, "I just like the idea of you calling me Lady Grey in your head or writing it down in that diary of yours."

She must never know.

"It's Caitlyn, by the way. Caitlyn Grey. And yes, I am Caitlyn Grey of Grey Enterprises. Or I guess Lady Grey of Grey Enterprises. Whichever floats your boat."

I managed to calm myself down a little, "Wow. Your family is one of the most powerful in all of Minecraftia. Your factories have made some of the most powerful technologies ever seen."

"Yup, and now it's all gone," she leaned back in her chair, "the Ender King wiped it out in a single blast. My family's legacy, and my future. Gone. So I plan on finding that monster and smashing him right out of the sky."

Lady Grey, or I guess Caitlyn, then turned to look at me. "What about you, huh? You should have left by this point, so why in the Nether did you decide to stick around and help people?"

"Would you believe me if I told you I got a stomach ache every time I tried to *not* help people?"

She grinned, "Ah, the Hero's Bane."

"Come again?"

"Ask Darkmist about it, he'll tell you everything."

She glanced at her clock, "As for me, I need to head off to bed. If we're stealing an airship then I want to be well-rested."

She sauntered over to the door, "And by the way Axel, I'm sorry about what I said before. You were right to help those people."

I smiled, "Thank you."

She winked at me and departed for her room.

DAY 21

This is it. The big heist.

Darkmist is going over the plans in the other room. Lady Grey is sharpening her ax. I'm... writing in my diary, as you can probably guess.

I asked Darkmist about what the mayor meant by the prophecy's enchantment. He wasn't too sure, although he'd heard a rumor about it.

"I figured it was just an old tale, but apparently not. Supposedly, the prophecy prevents information 'leaking out'. You're not allowed to write down information concerning the prophecy. If you do, it'll slowly erase itself from the paper. Even audio recordings of people reading the prophecy quickly deteriorate."

"So then we either have to reach the prophecy itself or find one of the books relating to it?" I asked him.

"Seems like it. I believe the books were written by the original author of the prophecy, so they're not affected by the enchantment. Still, we won't need them if we make it to Skytown."

If. It's a big if at that. Lady Grey's spies confirmed this morning that Mayor McBlockers posted extra guards around the airships. Plus, the power plant is on lockdown, meaning her spies can't even shut down the Redstone dispensers. The mission just got fifty times harder...

And yet, everyone seems to be okay with it.

Darkmist is happily humming along to his plans. Lady Grey is whistling a tune. Heck, even I feel just fine. I shouldn't, because I'm about to undertake some dangerous mission which could very well cost me my life. But honestly? I've never felt more alive.

I've come to realize just how dull my existence was. Slaving away in a library for days on end, sometimes not even venturing out into the sunlight. It was boring and monotonous, I just figured it was for me because some guy at a party laughed and told me I wasn't meant to be a hero.

Well, look who's laughing now.

Alright, looks like we're about to head out. Wish me luck diary. We're gonna need it.

Later…

That…

That was something.

Just after we left the inn, we ran into some trouble. A couple of the city guards approached us, warrants in their hands.

"Axel Silverblade, Hero Darkmist, Lady Caitlyn Grey, I'm sorry but we have reason to suspect you're about to commit a crime."

Darkmist reached for his blade, but I held my hand up. "Come on guys, you know that's not true."

"Sorry, but this is on the mayor's orders. I don't have much of a choice here.

I shrugged, "You could just pretend you didn't see us."

One of the guards, a young fellow in a chainmail helmet, opened his mouth to protest. The other cottoned on and silenced his colleague.

"I mean, I guess you did just save a bunch of people from the clutches of the Flayer," he mused, "guess that warrants enough for us to turn our heads for about… thirty seconds."

Darkmist nodded, "Much appreciated."

With that, we departed into the alleyways, sinking into the shadows before they could change their minds.

"Nicely done," Lady Grey ruffled my hair, "now all we have to do is reach the airstrip an-"

Her words died in her throat, just like the sunlight. An immense shadow leaked its way across the city, covering the entirety of Airstrip Delta in a single breath. We froze in place, our eyes drawn upwards towards the clouds that were beginning to part...

The Ender King descended. Monstrous in length and monstrous in looks. Hundreds of glowing red eyes bore their gaze down upon the city, each teeming with malice and cruelty. Tentacles hung loosely from its body, twitching back and forth. Its head was nothing more than a giant oculus, casting its gaze upon the helpless citizens below.

"By all that is holy..." Darkmist muttered, "we have to go now."

I looked back at the citizens, who were rushing for shelter wherever they could find it. I reached towards them, but Lady Grey grabbed me.

"Axel, you can't help them this time. You know that."

I grunted, my chest burning as I refused to acknowledge the Hero's Bane. Even so, I accepted it and turned away from them. Lady Grey offered me a sympathetic smile.

"We'll save them, I promise. But right now we need to beat the Ender King."

"Y-yeah," I managed to push out from my hoarse throat.

And so, we kept on running. The Ender King hadn't launched his assault yet, but it wouldn't be long now. When he destroyed Jebville, he'd floated in the sky only long enough to get a quick look at the town. How long before he rained wanton destruction on the city? Seconds? Minutes?

We approached Airstrip Delta itself. An Obsidian wall surrounded the facility, the only opening offered to us was through an iron gate. Guards manned the walls with dispensers and bows, but right now their focus was leeched by the arrival of the Ender King. We had to use this moment of distraction.

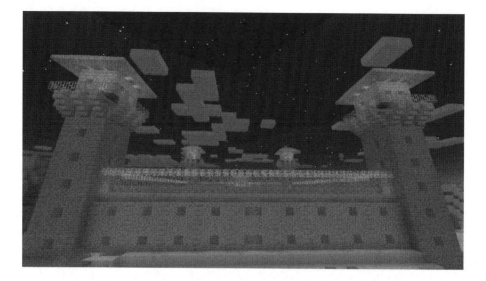

The walls of Airship Delta.

At the wall, Darkmist grabbed me and quickly tossed me to the top. A single guard caught sight of me and drew his blade. I unsheathed me own and disarmed him with a single swipe. He opened his mouth, a yelp forming. Instead, Lady Grey grabbed him. She covered his mouth and delivered a swift chop, knocking him unconscious.

We dropped down, having cleared the first obstacle. Ahead was the airfield, where a few airships were being refueled. Most were too small to suit our needs, but one did catch our eye. A large vessel armed with a couple of arrow dispensers, well-shielded from harm with its iron hull.

"That's the one," I motioned. The other two agreed.

"We'll need something sturdy to get us to Skytown," Darkmist noted.

Then, an explosion.

A short distance away, a cobblestone house melted to glass. The hundred-and-one eyes of the Ender King began their assault. Purple jets blinked from the eyes, slamming into streets, homes, and stores. Heat wafted into my face as fires sprang up across the city, the smell of burning charcoal assaulting my nose. Then, the screams followed.

"Come on," Darkmist grabbed my arm and pulled me forward. Lady Grey followed, drawing her ax.

"HEY, YOU, STOP!"

One of the guards shouted but we paid no mind, focusing our attention ahead. Two dispensers dislodged themselves from the ground, whirring into action and deploying their load of arrows. Darkmist replied with a shield, absorbing the brunt of their assault, as I tossed a bucket of water at the devices. The liquid wiped the Redstone out, leaving the dispensers non-functional.

"I'll get the maps we need," Darkmist ran towards the central building, a tall tower with a magnificent spire affixed to the top. We focused on the airship, currently being loaded by a few workers. They soon spotted us and dropped their gear, arming themselves with the scarce tools they had. From the corner of my eye, I spotted three guards armed in diamond making their way towards us as well.

I focused on the closest worker, a young lad with bright red hair. I knocked his spanner aside and shoved him to the ground. He scampered. I raced towards the airship as Lady Grey dispensed of the other two, scaring them off. She searched the ground for something, her calm face melting to panic.

"There's no keycard," she confirmed as she boarded the airship.

"Wait, what!?"

"I'll have to hack it," she shrugged, "but that's gonna take a minute. You'll need to deal with the guards."

Dang it. I grabbed Lady Grey's ax and descended the airship once more. There I was greeted by the three guards, their enchanted swords pointed at me.

"Step off the ship and surrender, nobody needs to get hurt."

"We're trying to save the world!" I countered, "I think you can spare an airship for that precise reason."

"A likely story," one of the guards laughed, but another gave me a funny look.

"Say... you're the guy who saved all those people from the Flayer, ain't' ya?"

I nodded, "And now we're trying to stop the Ender King, but we can only do it if we get to Skytown."

They turned to look at the Ender King. The city was burning up like a barbecue. Surges of flame consumed wood and cobble buildings alike, melting them into mush. A horrific cloud of smoke choked the skies above the city, a dark cloud bringing with it a storm of finality.

"How are you gonna stop that?" One of the guards sneered at me, "Huh? You don't look much like a hero."

He was right of course. I didn't have the coolness factor of Darkmist's costume, nor the calm fierceness that Lady Grey wore like a mask. Looking down at my clothes, I saw I was still dressed in my regular librarian's outfit. Smart, dignified and yet marred with scratches and burns. The wear and tear of a journey that shifts you from what you were to something new.

"Heroes come in all different shapes and sizes," I replied, "just the other week I was a librarian, happy to enjoy my life in peace and quiet."

"So you haven't even been a hero all that long?" The guard who mocked me, a fellow with an eyepatch and an exhausted expression on his face, just shook his head. "You're the hope for this world?"

"I'm the best you've got," I told him, plain and simple. "I might not look like much, but I did save those people. I've fought the Flayer twice, and come out of it mostly unscathed. I've journeyed halfway over a broken world just to get here. You're looking for a hero? You could do a lot worse than me."

That gave them pause for thought. They glanced to each other, mulling my words. Was it enough to convince them? To turn them from this course of action and allow us safe passage out of the city? The wait felt like hours, and throughout it, all the city burned behind them.

"Well, I guess we can let you g-"

"COME ON LAD!" A roar came out from overhead.

I looked to the skies, where Darkmist emerged from the central tower. Between his teeth, he clutched a map. He leaped from the window and landed perfectly next to the airship. He attempted a casual lean against the hull of the ship, waving the map at me.

"Let's go. We've got an airship to steal."

Oh for the love o-

"GET THEM!" The guards yelled.

"Oops," Darkmist laughed, tossing down a smoke bomb.

The guards coughed and spluttered as we boarded the vessel, pulling up the ramp behind us. The interior was cramped and a little musky, but based on the design she'd be a swift ship that'd break us free from the grips of this doomed city.

"How are you doing?" Darkmist asked as he approached the front of the vessel.

"Almost there," Lady Grey replied as she pulled a few wires around. "And... done!"

The vessel hummed into existence. The metal hull lifted to life beneath us, gliding away on the wings of electricity. Lady Grey seated herself into the pilot's seat, flicking a few switches. We lurched upwards, slowly, the engines struggling to lift off so quickly.

"Come on, come on," I remember muttering to myself, my eyes shut tight.

"GRRRRRRR!" Lady Grey growled, and with a terrific roar pulled back on the controls and launched us skyward.

I grasped one of the handholds, gripping with all my strength as we took to the air. Below us, the guards shrank to tiny specks, followed closely by the airstrip itself. For a moment, my spirit lifted and I felt relieved. We'd done it. We'd escaped.

Then I got a look at the devastation below us. Ruined buildings gave the feel of a ghost town. Ant-like humans ran about, looking for shelter. The Ender King loomed over them, vaporizing anything that stumbled into its all-knowing gaze. One by one, the screams grew a little quieter...

And that burning feeling in my gut? It faded away into nothing, falling out of existence like it never existed, leaving only a parody of itself behind:

Disappointment.

DAY 22

It's been a rough journey, but we're keeping it together. Somehow.

Don't have much time to write at the moment. Been helping Lady Grey with navigation. She's been directing my attention to the map. I've been directing her around swarms of Ender Wyverns, which are clogging up the skies right now.

We saw another airship go down, not too far from ours. Those little demons are like vicious crows. They tore and ripped into the hull of that ship, sending it plummeting before we could do anything. Lady Grey flew us into a cloud formation, making sure we wouldn't be caught up in the struggle.

We're about a third of the way to Skytown, although we've made a bit of a startling discovery. Looks like one of the fuel cells was hit during the escape. We've got enough to make it halfway, but unless we find a charging dock somewhere in the skies then we're in big trouble.

Lady Grey wants me at the wheel again. I'll write more tomorrow.

DAY 23

Yeah, the situation is looking graver by the second.

We're running on fumes. Lady Grey's managed to drain every last bit of energy from that power cell, but in a couple of hours, we're done for. Normally the skies are full of charging docks, places where we can land to charge up our vehicles. The trouble is they've all been destroyed. If the Ender King and the Flayer control the ground, then the Ender Wyverns control the skies. They've destroyed every platform we've come across.

Still, the good news is that we've had clear skies for the past couple of hours, with no Ender Wyverns in sight. We might have reached an area which they haven't visited yet, but I'm not sure. We'll just need to keep flying and see what we can find.

I also had a chat with Darkmist, about something Lady Grey mentioned, the Hero's Bane.

He looked at me with big, sparkling eyes, almost like he was impressed. "Ah, so it did get passed down the Silverblade line. I'll admit, I was worried you didn't have it."

"Well, what is it?" I asked as we stood on the deck of the airship, watching the twinkling of a twilight sky.

"A feeling," he explained, "this burning in your gut that tells you to enact justice wherever necessary."

"Sounds... kinda dangerous," I pointed out, "what if it was an unwinnable situation."

"Trust me, Axel, heroes have to face them all the time. And sometimes, they don't walk away. Just look at what happened in Jebville. A lot of heroes didn't get out of there. But the whole point of being a hero is to risk yourself in those situations."

"Not sure I like the sound of that."

True enough, my gut was tightening at the mere mention of it. Giving my life up for the greater good? Sure I took some risks, what with helping those people and saving them from the Flayer. But throwing my life on the line? The Hero's Bane faltered, shuddered at the very thought like my resolve was being questioned. Was I really cut out to be a hero?

"Hey, look," Darkmist patted me on the back, "most of the time, we heroes walk away. It's in our name, after all. We're here to save the world, to protect it from the forces of evil. So don't worry too much about things. Chances are you won't ever have to face a situation like that anyway. Just stick behind me and things will be alright."

"I hope so," I muttered.

Risking my life… the possibility of death. It wasn't something I saw often in my career as a librarian. There was only that one time when a bookshelf nearly fell on top of me. Thankfully I rolled out of the way at the last second. Well, I say rolled. I mean I dived out of the way. But close enough comparison. Risking my life to save Minecraft though.

Well, I guess it's something I've been doing for the past few days. I mean, look at where we've ended up at the moment. Sitting in a floating coffin, just waiting for it to plummet back down to earth.

This isn't good. We *need* to get to Skytown. The longer we take, the longer the rest of Minecraftia suffers. The airship was the only means we had to make it there but…

Jeez, I don't know anymore. I'm getting more and more worried by the second.

And...

Wait.

Crud. Ender Wyverns. THEY'VE SPOTTED US!

DAY 24

Lost in forest. Supplies low.

No sign of Lady Grey or Darkmist.

Monsters in the shadows. This is a bad place.

Hearing voices. Will write later.

DAY 25

Okay, sorry about my ramblings in the last entry there. I've got a few things to explain since our last meeting, my dear diary.

As you probably gathered, we got hit by Ender Wyverns. Good news is that there weren't too many of them and by working together, we managed to fight them off. Working as a group we drove them away with arrows, forced them into a specific spot and fired the TNT Cannon at them. Blew them all to Kingdom Come.

And it was at that precise moment the airship ran out of power, beginning its slow yet accelerating descent to the earth below us.

Lady Grey managed to steer us to a forest area, where she looked for a safe spot to set the airship down. Of course, the entire area was covered in dang trees, so there really wasn't much of a safe spot. Still, by gum, she actually pulled it off. Managed to fit just between two tight trees and land in some clearing. Lemme tell you, she rocked.

Rocked hard enough to throw me over the side.

I spent an entire day as a savage. Roaming the woods in search of food, hunting prey with only a makeshift stick and learning to avoid the predators which roam these lands. You're not gonna believe it but there are creepers here!

That only lasted for a day, however. It turns out that the voices I was hearing were actually Darkmist and Lady Grey, enjoying a campfire just a few blocks away from me. I thought it was some fire demon, out to consume my soul. Nope, just my traveling companions. They found me a few hours ago and restored me to my regular sanity.

Turns out the jungle is no place for a librarian.

We talked our options over.

"Any chance of finding a new fuel cell?" I asked Lady Grey.

She thought about it, "Maybe... The fuel cell is powered by a mixture of gunpowder, Glowstone dust and a sprinkling of Redstone. If you could find all of that then we could just recharge ours and head off."

"Easier said than done," said Darkmist, "the gunpowder is easy. This place is teeming with creepers."

As if to accentuate this, an explosion went off in the distance.

"The problem is finding the other two objects. Forests like this often have temples at the heart of them. Provided it wasn't looted it might contain the things we're looking for. Yet even if we a vein of Redstone, we don't have the tools to dig it out. And I don't know about you guys, but I do NOT fancy a trip to the Nether to find some Glowstone dust."

"That's why we have to hope there's some here," I said, "we can't build a Nether portal with the tools we have, nor do we have the means to venture into it if we did."

"Yeah, no offense Axel but the Nether really wouldn't be for you," Lady Grey said, "even if we could go there. The monsters in that place would tear you apart."

"None taken," I replied honestly, "they'd burn up all of my books. So let's stick to finding Glowstone here."

"Alright," Darkmist nodded, "that means venturing into the heart of this place and finding the temple."

"If it's all the same to you guys, I'll stay with the ship," Lady Grey offered, "someone has got to protect it. If the creepers find it and damage it, we're not leaving."

113

"Good idea. Axel and I will pack some supplies and find this temple as swiftly as we can."

Lady Grey brought out a crate of resources. She sorted through it with her blocky hands, handing us a few pieces of meat and three bottles of water each. "Don't go dying out in those woods, I'd hate to know I wasted this delicious food."

"I'll try my best," I laughed.

Darkmist gave her a quick high-five before departing into the woods, leaving me with Lady Grey.

"Erm, hey," I waved.

"Yo," she replied back.

"So..."

"So indeed..."

My heart beat away in my tightening chest. My words clambered desperately to emerge from my throat, yet every time they were forced back by a swallow of awkwardness. I instead replaced my silenced request with a small cough, waved at Lady Grey and headed after Darkmist.

"Not gonna lie Axel," Darkmist shook his head whilst laughing, "I could feel the cringe even from over here."

"Be quiet," I sighed, sulking as we began our trip into the forest.

Later…

Well, we've covered plenty of ground but no sign of the temple yet.

Not too far from the crash site, I stumbled upon a set of stone stairs leading downward. I pointed it out to Darkmist, and together we searched this small little bunker. Formed from iron blocks, our steps rang out in this hollowed home. The stench of rusted iron beat my nose, as we searched the clearly abandoned shelter.

"Nothing," Darkmist sighed as he closed the chest, "no Redstone or Glowstone."

The good news is that we have our gunpowder. We spotted a lone creeper lazily swaying in the sun, and decided to make our move.

"It's been a while since I actually fought any creepers," Darkmist explained, "but the principle is still the same. Run up to it, knock it back, switch to your partner.

Rinse, repeat. No heroics, no funny business. Even the toughest of heroes know to be careful around them."

"Got it," I promised.

We approached slowly, yet its keen ears swiftly detected our silent footsteps. It waddled over to us, its body bouncing between green and white. A low hiss dripped from its tongue, promising all kinds of pain if we didn't take it down.

"Alright," Darkmist drew his sword, "STRIKE!"

He dived forward, landing an uppercut on the creeper. It fell backward, growling as it did. It struggled to its feet, the urge to explode intensifying. We stepped backward, allowing it to calm down.

"Your turn!"

"STRIKE!" I yelled, slicing the creeper across the belly and kicking it back into the water.

"Nice," Darkmist grinned, "if it explodes then the water will absorb most of the impact."

Luckily (or perhaps unluckily depending on your point of view), it didn't. One final slash from Darkmist and the creeper exploded into a puff of smoke, leaving a few piles of grey dust floating in the water.

"Always wondered how this never got wet," Darkmist mused, slipping it into his backpack.

"How many more creepers do we need to take down?" I asked.

"Five or six. Should net us more than enough."

And so our hunt continued. Over the next couple of hours, we struggled to track and separate creepers from their herds, trying not to attract dozens at a time. Yet with careful patience and fine swings of our blade, soon we had half a dozen fallen creepers behind us.

"Not bad," Darkmist nodded, "you're getting good. Less dumb luck and more actual skill."

"Thanks."

"Keep it up and we might have to make you an official hero when we get back."

"The library will miss me."

"Yeah, but the world would miss you more. I think you're made for this sort of thing."

"Yeah, maybe..."

We ventured a little deeper into the jungle, Darkmist leaving a trail of objects behind us to mark our way. Yet despite our progress, there was no sign of the temple. No ancient markings of stone, no old roads dug up by civilizations long since fallen, nothing...

And as we carried on, I began to feel it. There was an... emptiness to this place. The sense of something missing. When I crossed over certain blocks, the feeling grew stronger. Like once upon a time the life and the air had been sucked right out of that space. Darkmist didn't say anything, but I feel like he felt it too. He had this look in his eyes, behind that clothed face. He'd occasionally mutter to himself and twitch uncomfortably. Heck, even a few creepers that dared to stalk us refused to go near those spots.

We've stopped for the night, but we've already exhausted most of our supplies. If we don't find this place tomorrow, I think we're done for.

Those aren't the kind of words I want to be writing here, diary. But I've got to be honest with myself. After all, a hero is supposed to risk his life, right? I just thought it wouldn't end here, a million blocks from home, in the heart of this barren jungle.

DAY 26

No sign of the temple.

It's getting worse.

We finished off most of our supplies by lunchtime. Rather than venture back, we decided to continue on. After all, what would be the point of going back to the airship? There are no more supplies there unless by some miracle Lady Grey has got a farm going and has single-handedly found a way to cook creeper meat.

But what are the chances of that?

Those empty zones, they're growing more frequent now. Still, perhaps that's also a source of hope? Are we growing close to the center of what caused all of these? If so, will we find supplies there? Is it perhaps at the heart of this curse where the temple sits? Darkmist thinks I sound insane, but he hasn't ventured back from this course yet.

He's probably right though. And whatever we're heading towards, it can't be anything good.

Oh, and to fire the final arrow into this pinata of misery, I'm almost out of ink. Meaning I won't even able to document how things come to an end. I'm hoping I might stumble upon some squid in a small pool of water, though the chances of that are slim to none. When was the last time you heard of a squid appearing in a small pool of water? When was the last time you heard of a squid appearing anywhere?

Like I mentioned all that time ago, mobs disappeared. Yet here, they exist. At least, creepers do. This place is different from the rest of Minecraft, and it's only through that solitary hope that I'm pushed onward to find a way out of this mess.

That, and the burning feeling of the Hero's Bane in my gut commanding me to find a way out of this jungle and to keep fighting the forces of evil.

We're gonna rest for a little bit. The ink's just about to run out anyway. If by some miracle this journal has another page, then you'll know we succeeded. Otherwise, this is Axel Silverblade, signing off.

Later...

We found it...

I... I don't even know what we found. The things we saw, the images burned into my head, they're all mixed up. Like someone took a perfectly formed puzzle and threw it against the wall, the pieces scattering all over the place.

I think I'll be musing over some of the things I saw in there for the rest of my life. For now, though, let's see if I can piece it together to form a coherent journal entry.

First things first, we're alive. We did find the Glowstone dust and the Redstone. When we made it back to the airship, we were expecting to find the place in ruins and Lady Grey to have passed on from starvation...

Guess who managed to get a farm going and discover a way to cook creeper meet? Yup, Lady Grey did.

She waved us over once she saw us, offered our weary bodies some food and took the supplies from our still shocked bodies. A few minutes later and she had a recharged power cell, all juiced up and ready to go.

We've been flying at full speed for the past hour. Those two are adamant on reaching Skytown as quickly as possible. Too much time was wasted in that blasted jungle, and we need to get back on track to saving the world.

Yet, was that time wasted among those trees?

The things we saw, the sights we experienced... That thing we fought.

Alright, buckle up because it was quite the adventure down there.

We discovered the temple. We pushed on through those empty, hollow places and just as I said, we found the temple at the heart of it. Yet immediately, Darkmist noticed something was up.

"These temples were built to stand for the ages," he explained, "you almost always find them on the surface, or maybe partially buried, but always plainly visible. They become part of the world, they don't get swallowed by it."

He pointed to the structure, "So what in Jeb's name is this thing doing buried halfway into the earth?"

Sure enough, the temple had sunk. It sat in the bowl of a crater, surrounded by blackened earth. A few scant creepers inhabited this strange new world, yet as we grew closer they saw fit to ignore us and turn their attention elsewhere. That hollowness rang deeper into my chest, beaten into me under the steady smacking of my heart. A grating whistling nailed its way into my eardrums, and more than once I found myself stopping to rest.

"What on Minecraftia is this place?" I asked.

"A place where everything once living is now dead," he replied mysteriously.

Didn't really answer my question. Still, I got the gist of what he meant. Was this the battleground of some ancient conflict? The graveyard of fallen heroes? Or was it something else? I pushed the thoughts into the "review later" pile in my brain, and we completed our descent into the crater.

A set of stairs awaited us, a dusty red carpet to all the horrors lurking below. Together, we descended. Darkmist lit the way with a torch, and I guided us with the light of my iron blade, searching the shadows for any shape of foe or monstrosity. Yet there were none to be found. Only cobwebs nuissanced us, and they were no match for my sharp edge.

As we reached the end of the steps, our footsteps echoed loudly, rebounding off stone and metal. We passed through an old door and find ourselves paying tribute to what had once been a throne room. Smoke stained banners hung from the walls, their fabrics wafting a faint burning smell. Water gently dripped in the distance, a quiet jester heralding our arrival. Yet the true symbol of royal authority was the black throne at the far-end of this hallowed hall. Unmarked, unblemished and seething with the hatred of a dark king's specter.

Behind me, I could hear Darkmist rummaging through a few chests. Yet my attention had been drawn elsewhere. My eyes were focused on that black, iron throne. Images formed in my head, flashing through my mind like speeding Minecarts. In every one of them, I was seated upon the throne, a warped crown atop my head. And all of them ended the same way: a great burst of light, scorching the palace clean.

One step at a time, I approached the vast seat. My hand extended outwards, yearning to brush the smooth material. My vision tunneled, burrowing towards a solitary target. That throne. I grew closer and closer. My breath hitched. Eyes wide. Chest tight. My very being screamed to set itself upon the throne like I was the last piece in some great, complex puzzle.

"Woah, easy there," Darkmist grabbed me and shook me.

The trance was broken. My eyes focused on my mentor, who smiled at me and held up two items: Redstone and Glowstone dust.

"Turns out those chests were full of treasures. Come on, let's get out of here."

The feeling was weakened, but ever-present. Numbly hanging the back of my mind, the throne tempting me with its secrets. Yet I denied it. Before leaving, however, I did spot something in the corner of the room.

A staircase. Hidden off to the side, like its architect wanted it to be unnoticed. I pointed it out to Darkmist, who eyed it curiously.

"Don't know if we should be spending any more time here than necessary."

"Might be something useful here," I said. "This place is ancient, and something happened here a long time ago. Who knows when we might be able to return?"

Darkmist sighed, "I've got a bad feeling about this."

Together, we descended the twisting staircase. Cobwebs threatened to slow us, but a swipe of my sword later and they were cast aside. Despite its age, a couple of eternal torches hung from the walls, giving off a faint glow. I took one of them in my hand, and we continued down the spiral passage.

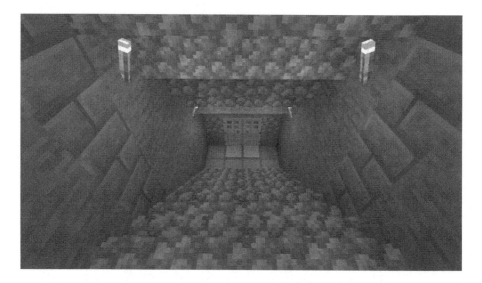

The stairs, leading to the depths of this place...

At the bottom, we were greeted by an iron door. No mechanism was in place to open it, but a quick smack of the pickaxe and nothing remained to block our way. The pathway instead opened up to a grand chamber. The dusty ceiling extended up at least fifteen to twenty blocks. Ahead sat another staircase leading up to some great altar. Atop it stood a thin column, brushing against a ceiling of obsidian.

"This is... strange," Darkmist looked around the room, "I've heard rumors about these places but never thought they actually existed."

"What is it?"

"An old place. A powerful place. One of the remnants of a bygone era. And I'm not mistaken..."

He stepped over to a plaque hanging at the base, its words marred from an era of age. He scrubbed at the dust with his hand, eventually removing enough to make it legible once more. The words were in some ancient tongue that I wasn't familiar with, but Darkmist seemed to have no problem with it.

"To those who dwell above, please accept our humblest apologies... Not our intention to use it... The Great Devourer left us with no option... please forgive us."

Darkmist stepped back, scratching his head. "Yup, it's a weapon alright. An ancient one at that."

"You know it?"

"Only from mentions in ancient scrolls. There were always rumors about these artefacts existing, but it was never really proven. There was no sign of these weapons. At least, not until now."

"The Great Devourer," I thought about it, "that's got to be the Ender King, right?"

"Oh without a doubt. We know he existed at some point during the ancient times, so this is probably what they used to defeat him."

"So let's fire it off right now, put an end to him before he can cause any more damage."

"Not that simple kiddo. The Ender King probably knows about the existence of these weapons, especially if they beat him the first time around. It wouldn't surprise me if he took some precautions."

Darkmist leaned back against the altar, "And even if we could use them against him, think of the devastation. That plaque mentions an apology for a reason. These weapons are probably some of the most dangerous on the planet. And that empty feeling on the surface? This weapon had something to do with it, I'm sure."

I take another look at the structure, at the obsidian covering on the ceiling above. "Was it ever fired though? It looks like they blocked off the passageway to the surface."

"Not that's an intriguing one," Darkmist climbed the steps for a closer look, "perhaps the work of someone who created the weapon? Maybe he was shocked at the damage his creation did, and so he made sure that it could never be done again?"

"Maybe," I thought about it but I wasn't convinced by such an easy explanation. "That throne room... did you have any weird feelings?"

"Not one," Darkmist shook his head, "well aside from the creepiness. Why, was something bothering you about it?"

I hesitated. Should I tell Darkmist the truth? How would he react to knowing I had a vision pop into my head, showing me strange images of memories that weren't my own? Would he call me mad? Would he be understanding? Or would he question my sanity and order me back to the ruins of my home?

"Nevermind, I was just a bit weirded out as well."

"I feel you," he said, as we ascended the steps to the top of the altar, "this place has that feeling about it. Honestly, I'm impressed you made it through that field of emptiness, to begin with. A lesser man might have balked at the sight of it. But you made it through."

"My gut might have been pretty mad at me if I didn't," I laughed.

"The Hero's Bane... you know it's something you can learn to control eventually, right?"

"That so?"

"Yeah," Darkmist stroked his chin, "though as you grow as a hero, you'll also be seeking bigger challenges. The Bane will probably grow in power as well, demanding you take on bigger challenges and that you resolve them quickly. It's something we need to learn to control."

"Sounds like it could be the cause of some real trouble down the line."

Darkmist paused for a moment, "Well yeah, especially for a Silverblade."

"Eh?"

"Your dad never mentioned this to you?"

I shook my head, "I didn't even know about the Hero's Bane until a short time ago."

"Right, of course. Well supposedly, the Hero's Bane afflicts Silverblades more than regular heroes."

"Oh..."

But the moment he mentioned it, a lot of things started making sense in my head. My dad going to slay the Ender Dragon, my grandfather exploring the Nether, my great grandfather taking on invincible warriors like Darkmist... They were just seeking to sate the Hero's Bane. To quench that overwhelming desire to do good.

"But we can control it, right?"

"Yeah, with practice," Darkmist nodded, "although I've never known a Silverblade to try. The life of a hero is in their blood."

"But I never felt the need for it before."

"Yeah, but it's something you have to activate. You deciding to become a hero is what did it. There's probably still time for you to walk away from all of this and to allow the Bane to settle, but if you continue down the path then you will be pushed to much greater heights, and demanded to take on greater foes."

"What foe is greater than the Ender King?" I asked with a shaking voice.

But Darkmist just sighed, "The Hero's Bane doesn't operate like that. It'll demand stronger."

And before I could delve further into this mystery, we made it to the very top of the altar. Here the pillar thrummed, giving off a hazing aura that enveloped the summit of this miniature temple. My legs wobbled at its mere presence, and I had to remind myself that the weapon wasn't about to activate on its own.

"You're fine," I muttered, "everything is gonna be fine."

"Who dares to disturb this place?"

Uh-oh.

At that moment, we were greeted by a specter. A wisp of white and grey, descending from the ceiling and joining us atop the altar. A robed man wielding an ancient sword, his gaze drifted from me to Darkmist, a pair of empty blue eyes piercing into our very being.

"We're not here to trouble you," Darkmist said, "we just wanted to look around."

"You 'just wanted to look around' one of the most powerful weapons in Minecraftia's history?"

"Pretty much," Darkmist nodded, "anyways we'll be going now."

"So you can siege this place with your armies and attempt to seize the weapon for yourself?" The specter pointed its blade at Darkmist, "I think not."

Darkmist knocked the sword aside with his own. Together, we pointed our weapons at the spirit, who chuckled.

"My, a challenge. Guarding this place had become quite the bore. I trust my skills aren't too rusty."

Spoiler alert: They weren't.

He immediately hit us with a flurry of slashes. His sword twisting through the air like a conductor's baton, controlling the flow of battle. Two strikes to me, three to Darkmist. We were shoved back to the edge, threatening to fall off. The spirit pushed forward. A lunge. We sidestepped, hoping he would fall. He instead hovered, coming back around and cutting low. Together, we barely stalled his advance.

"Tough cookie," Darkmist panted. The fight had only just begun and he was exhausted.

"We can take him," I huffed, the Hero's Bane flaring up at the challenge, "for Minecraftia!"

I cried out and stepped forward, bringing my weapon down upon his form. He slipped to the left, aiming to cut my exposed arm. Darkmist had me covered, bouncing the weapon back. The guardian slashed three times, two cuts from the left, one from the right. Darkmist's blade was knocked aside. He stabbed once more. I parried for Darkmist.

Alone, this fight would have been impossible. Together, however, we held our own.

Darkmist retrieved his weapon, throwing a makeshift ax from his back. The spirit deflected. A mistake. We came down on him like a surge of water, striking from two directions. He turned his blade vertically, just managing to catch both our attacks. But Darkmist pushed on. The flow of battle was his now.

Equipping a dagger, he brought down a storm of blows. Left. Right. Uppercut. Right again. Feint right, slash to the left. His speed picked up, to the point where I could no longer follow the direction and instead only watch in ax at the blurs left around him. Like trails of ice cutting against rings of fire, their solid forms hanging momentarily in the air, before melting to nothingness. Pulling back to reform, then striking with a cold fury once again.

I joined my blows to Darkmist's, our swords weaving a duet. Sheets of ice became blizzards of winter that swept over the specter's defenses and left him cold, frozen and open to our attacks. Our blades entwined, we struck with a powerful blow...

And cut into nothingness.

"My," the spirit huffed a short distance away, "you are formidable opponents... but you fight with a certain nobility. A justness seen only in the hearts of the true. I see now you did not come here for the weapon."

He lowered our blades, and he did the same. "This weapon... it was a mistake to unleash it upon the world. A mistake that we have paid dearly for."

"I don't suppose you can tell us what happened?" I asked, but he shook his head.

"We are forbidden from speaking it. A spell to protect knowledge, but one that has transformed into a curse. We are not allowed to warn those who would try to use it, for fear of imparting the knowledge of the weapon's creation. Instead, we might only defend its secrets from those who would attempt to yield them."

"You used it against the Great Devourer, a creature which has returned to the world," Darkmist said, "but from what you have said, I'm guessing the weapon is unsafe to use?"

The specter said nothing. Part of the curse, I'd guess. He could only stare on in solemn contemplation.

"We won't use it then. We'll find another way to defeat the Great Devourer."

"I... wish you luck in that regard," the specter smiled, "we did not find another way to do so. I pray that you have different luck."

He faded into nothingness after that, and we returned back to the staircase. Yet my eye was caught by something, lingering on one of the skeletons.

"An old journal," I swiped the dust from the front cover. Torn, beaten and sheathed full of pages of varying sizes. The mad ramblings of the court jester? Or something else? I pocketed it anyway, making my way back to the airship alongside Darkmist.

"Something troubles me," Darkmist admitted as we were halfway back.

"What is it?"

"The Prophecy of the Dark King has existed for as long as Skytown. It was birthed in the earliest days of the world..."

"So?"

"So if it contains the secret to stopping the Ender King, why wasn't it used?"

That's a question I've been pondering since I got back to the ship. One that worries me greatly...

Phew, my hand is cramping. I don't know how else to continue this. Those images though... The ones I saw back in the throne room... How do I describe it to you? Never in my life have I been seated on a throne like that, nor was I responsible for something that threatened to wipe out an entire royal building. But they felt so real... The sight of me on that throne almost felt like a familiar memory. A distant memory I'd long hoped to forget.

I dunno if I should talk with the others about this. They might think I'm insane. No, better to just leave it and forget about it for the time being. It was probably nothing important anyway. For now, let's put an end to this adventure.

Onwards, to Skytown!

DAY 27

Maybe I've come to expect too much from this adventure.

The good news is that we made it to Skytown. Lady Grey called us both on deck that very morning. There in the distance, illuminated by the scorching sun, was the floating city. Great turbines, silently yet steadily, held the wondrous city in place. Hovering gently, about twenty-thousand blocks above the surface. If this city was ever to come tumbling down, oh boy, the devastation it would cause...

The incredible city of Skytown.

See, it's stuff like that. I'm almost thinking like an action hero now. I was expecting that upon arrival in Skytown, we'd be met with hordes of zombies or the Flayer and a bunch of Ender Wyverns. Heck, maybe the Ender King himself would show up to take down the city and reduce it to a burning wreck. None of that. Know what actually happened?

We got stuck in traffic for FOUR HOURS!

Yeah. Turns out we weren't the only people interested in Skytown. A lot of people are coming here. Darkmist managed to cut the line a little bit thanks to his hero credentials, and Lady Grey offered to bribe a few people, but we still ended up waiting a good long while. IN THE AIR! I saw one person's ship go down and people scrambled to steal his spot. We managed to take it for ourselves.

I was worried our fuel cells wouldn't withstand the wait, but Lady Grey (I need to start calling her Caitlyn) reassured me they'd be fine. That, and Darkmist was ready and waiting to steal another vehicle in case it came down to it. But eventually, we made it to the front of the line.

"Names please?" A bored-looking gentleman asked us.

"Darkmist the Hero," announced (who else?) Darkmist, "I travel with Axel Silverblade and Lady Caitlyn Grey. We have journeyed a vast distance, battling the forces of darkness in order to bring ourselves to your door to uncover the secret to saving the world."

"... Uh-huh," the exhausted intern nodded, "please wait here."

THIRTY MORE MINUTES! I don't know what the heck was going on, but we left suspended for another half-hour. People in the queue behind us started screaming and yelling, right until Lady Grey turned the TNT Cannon towards them and threatened to blast them straight out of the skies. They shut up after that.

Finally, the bored intern guy came back and handed me a little sticker to affix to the airship. With a gloomy nod he waved us on. Parking in Skytown wasn't much better but at least it wasn't a four-hour wait. After that we set ourselves up in one of the inns, where we've been relaxing ever since. Even though the world is at stake, Darkmist figured we all deserved a bit of a rest for the time being.

"Tomorrow we'll head over to the museum," he explained, "and resolve this mystery once and for all."

142

We milled around town for a bit, just passing the day by. Surprisingly, for all the people that came to Skytown, there was almost nobody here. The streets were deathly quiet, with not even the birds to sing for us. After visiting the third empty store it got kind of boring, so we dig a bit of fishing in the floating rivers, repaired our equipment at the smithy and headed back to the inn for dinner. By that point, even the innkeeper had decided to take a holiday.

"Is there something I'm not understanding?" I asked the other two after we were forced to help ourselves to the inn's kitchen. Don't worry, we left money on the counter.

"What's up?" Caitlyn asked. (Got it right this time.)

"Where is everybody?"

"Might be some holiday," Darkmist mused, "I have heard that Skytown enjoys some weird and bizarre traditions. Heck, they might even be playing tricks on the locals."

"Yeah," I played with my soup, "must be something like that."

DAY 28

Well diary, today's the day.

I don't have a whole lot of time to write at the moment, so I'll need to make this as snappy as possible. Lady Grey's already got her ax sharpened in case too many people get in her way at the museum, and Darkmist got us a private viewing with the prophecy. Honestly, I'm surprised he managed to find anyone at all.

Looks like this adventure will be coming to a close soon. But boy, it's been an absolute blast. The Flayer, the Abandoned Lands, all of it. Scary, yes? Fate of the world hangs in the balance? Also yes. But we did it. We made it to Skytown, and now we're gonna figure out just how to beat the Flayer. I'll write more soon but we're heading out, diary.

Can't wait for the next adventure!

Axel

I packed up my precious journal and slotted it neatly into my bag. Hoisting it over my back I joined the smiling Caitlyn and the proud Darkmist. Together, the three of us walked the cobble streets towards the museum.

"Empty streets again," I pointed out. The market stalls looked like they'd been abandoned. The food and tools had been left out to hang.

"Some practical joke," Lady Grey squinted her eyes, "this is getting to be a bit strange now."

"Relax," Darkmist waved his hand, "I've got a sixth sense for danger and I'm telling you that right now, we're fine."

"If you say so."

The streets shifted from cobble to iron. I wondered for a moment if anyone had ever tried to harvest them. Then again, looking at the dispensers positioned on the roofs of certain buildings, they wouldn't get very far if they tried. Just ahead of us stood the museum. Probably one of the most towering structures here, dwarfing even the Court of Skytown.

The Skytown museum.

"Hello?" Darkmist called out as we walked inside, "Mr. Curator? We spoke this morning?"

His voice bounced through the massive halls of the complex, but no answer rose to meet him.

"How'd you meet him?" I asked.

"Oh, a conversation over the phone."

This was getting stranger by the second. We waited around for a little but the curator was a total no show.

"Forget this," I motioned with my hand, "follow me and let's go find the prophecy ourselves."

The three of us headed down the hallway marked "PRIVATE – DO NOT ENTER!" A few white sheets were draped over some of the exhibits. One resembled a suit of armor, another the mummified remains of a villager. Caitlyn peeked under it and judging from the look on her face, there wasn't anything all that amazing underneath.

"My word," Darkmist laughed, "you've changed an awful lot. I bet you wouldn't have dreamed of entering the private section of a museum without permission when your journey began."

"Course not," I laughed, "although I do like the newfound... liberty, shall we say? I was way too uptight as a librarian."

We continued a little further. Here the dim lights gave way to shining Glowstone chandeliers, illuminating beautiful pieces of artwork. Paintings of Herobrine, color splotches of great battles, even depictions of the supposed creators of Minecraft. Wonderous stuff, all of it. I'd have loved more time to browse, but we were here for one specific piece.

"So where is it exactly?" Caitlyn asked.

"Up ahead," said Darkmist, "they keep a fake tablet on show for the tourists, but the real one rests down here."

"This is it," I smiled, "we can finally put an end to the Ender King."

"He's terrorized the good people of the realm for too long. This prophecy will be his undoing."

"I'm all on-board for that," Caitlyn nodded.

Finally, we came to a small iron door. Behind it sat a darkened chamber, with a single exhibit covered by a white blanket. The name over the door read "The Prophecy of the Dark King."

"At last," Darkmist smiled, "we've made it. Inside lies the knowledge we seek, the secrets we need to put an end to the Ender King."

He turned to both of us, "You two should be proud. You've done so much to bring us to this point, to help save the world. Lesser beings would have turned and run, but you guys stuck it out to the end."

"That Ender King owes me a new factory," said Caitlyn.

"I'm especially proud of you Axel," he pointed to me.

"Eh?" My cheeks reddened a little bit.

"You almost *did* turn tail and run, but in the end, you decided to see things through. You stuck it out, saved so many innocent people and managed to help get us here. I've got to thank you for that, for embracing your inner hero and bringing us to this point."

"It was nothing," I tried to step away from the awkwardness, "I'm just happy to have helped."

"Right, well with all that said and done..."

Darkmist entered the chamber, motioning for us to follow. "Come, let's figure out how we end this."

We made our way towards the tablet. The white blanket hung loose like it had been thrown over in a hurry. Dim Redstone lights flickered in the corners of the room, giving the place a very eerie feel. I briefly considered lighting a torch, but I didn't fancy explaining to the good citizens of Skytown that their museum went up in flames just because I couldn't see in the dark.

As grew closer, however, I could feel it. *A chill.* A certain coldness hanging in the air that left me cold to my core. The chill turned to nervousness, then to a punch in the gut. My legs carried me forward in a surge of speed, as I raced towards the white blanket and ripped it off...

"Oh no."

The Prophecy was in ruins. Where a magnificent stone tablet should have stood, now there were only shards of rock littering the ground. Most had been trampled into dust as if to erase any chance of recovery. Darkmist muttered a few spells. Then he shouted them. Nothing happened. The damage was done. The Prophecy of the Dark King was destroyed.

"We're too late."

Caitlyn slammed her ax into the wall, screaming out. She cut into the walls twice more, before removing her weapon and storming out of the room. Darkmist tried a few final spells, even though it was clear to me there was no fixing this situation. With a resigned expression, he left the chambers behind.

And then I was alone, staring up the remains of The Prophecy.

I didn't understand. How long had it been like this? Weeks? Months? Or was this a recent job? Thoughts of the empty village of Skytown came flooding back to me, and all at once I understood it. The disappearing villagers, the eerie nature to the town, and now the destruction of the Prophecy. It led to one indisputable fact.

"CAITLYN! DARKMIST!" I charged after them.

I needn't have bothered. I found them in the hallway, staring down the curator. A portly man with short stubby legs. His jaw flapped open and shut like a possessed mailbox, and his eyes seared a deep purple. A victim of the Flayer.

"He's taken over the whole town, hasn't he?" Darkmist asked.

"Without a doubt. We need to get out of here."

I turned to leave via another exit, only to be met by two more of the Flayed. A man and a woman, probably husband and wife. They marched towards us with joined hands and clenched teeth, yelling some chanting in an unknown language. I tore through my backpack, looking for a bucket or some water. Nothing, we'd left it all in our rooms. A stupid move.

This whole situation was stupid. We'd been too complacent. We should have suspected this from the very start. But we were careless, and now we could be paying for that mistake with our lives. With no other option, I charged the curator. He garbled some gibberish at me, right up until I planted my foot in his flabby stomach. I smacked him across the head, as gently as I could, and knocked him down to the ground. Our path was open.

We rushed back to the museum. A few lingering mind-zombies blocked our path, but the large, open room made it easy to skirt around them. One blocked the entrance. I tackled him, and we fell together. Down the museum steps and on to the iron road of Skytown. He crumpled beneath me, injured, and the Hero's Bane burned. *You're here to help these people, not to injure them.*

Skytown was... something else. Burning in a spectacular inferno. Whilst it had yet to spread to most of the buildings, already the palace was aflame. A rising tornado of fire and fury that threatened to cover the entire city in a maelstrom of destruction. In just a few minutes, Skytown would be nothing more than a burning wreck a-

Wait.

"Someone clearly doesn't want us to get out," Darkmist coughed, keeping low to the ground to avoid the smoke.

"We need to stop those flames," I said.

"WHAT!?"

"You're insane," Lady Grey glared at me, "this city is done for."

"There are innocent people here," I pointed out, "and there's another problem. What if Skytown falls?"

Darkmist considered it, reaching the same conclusion as me. "The flames could shutdown Skytown's air turbines. If Skytown crashes into the ground, the devastation will be unimaginable. The resulting explosion would cause more destruction than anything the Ender King could up with."

"That's probably his plan," Lady Grey finished, wheezing in the smoke. "Alright, I see your point. We need to stop this before it gets that far. Question is, how do we stop those flames?"

We moved away from the museum, the smoke growing to horrific levels. My eyes scanned the battered down and there, gleaming through the smoke like some silvery beacon of hope, was a water tower. Low enough to douse the town if it were to be broken, but high enough to avoid the scalding reach of the flames.

I led Darkmist and Caitlyn over to it, pushing past the brainwashed citizens who stood in our way. The smoke tore at my vision, a veil seeking to choke off my knowledge of the surrounding area. Even s,o my eyes searched the smog, looking for any sign of the Flayer. *He's here, lurking in the darkness. If we're not careful, he'll ambush us all.*

Underneath the tower, an old wooden hatch led to the interior. I climbed the ladder positioned beneath it, peering through the hatch to find our saving grace. Yet the water tower was just that. A tower. Dried up on the inside, with only offerings of rust to quench the thirsting city. The Hero's Bane screamed at me for another solution, as I slipped from the ladder.

"Dry as a skeleton," I said.

Lady Grey slammed her ax into the wooden supports of the tower, almost toppling it with that single blow. Darkmist focused on pushing back the growing crowds of villagers, their possessed eyes speaking of their desire for our demise. I turned away from the danger at hand, diving deep into my mind and searching for something, anything that could help us.

Those visions peeked above the surface. The memories of me seated upon that throne. I pushed them back down like I was trying to drown them, focusing on the matter at hand. The water tower was dry, which probably meant every other water source in the city was spent. Whether it was the Flayer or a side-effect of the inferno, I don't know. Didn't matter really.

The flames tickled at my skin first, then lapped at it with sharp, furious swipes. I pulled away from the growing inferno, my arm singed. The three of us moved to a safer spot, coughing and spluttering all the way. Tears dripped from my eyes, desperately trying to rid them of their new, smokey flavor. All the while my mind blasted through the hundreds of books I'd read during my time at the library. I dove deep, deep in the records of Skytown, all the stories, all the blueprints, all th-

THAT'S IT!

"Can you fly a city!?" I grabbed Caitlyn by the shoulders.

"W-wha?"

"A city. This city. Can you fly it?"

"W-well I haven't exactly tried, but I can fly anything."

"Okay, because we don't need someone who can fly it," I let go of her, "we need someone who can drop it into the ocean."

"..."

"Err," Darkmist attempted to interrupt. I didn't let him.

"There's no water in the city, so we can't put it out. But if we position the city above the ocean, then slow its descent into the water, we can extinguish the flames and free everyone from the Flayer's control!"

The two paused for a second. Given what I was proposing, they might even have paused for a minute to think things over. Yet their thinking time came to a sudden end, with a howl of malice that shattered glass windows and burrowed into our skulls. From a veil of shadow, the Flayer appeared before us. Robed, purple-eyed and armed with a thin black sword that thrummed with an orange glow.

"Run."

We took off in the opposite direction. The Flayer warped behind us, his teleports almost bringing him within striking distance each time he used it. More than once Darkmist flipped round to parry a blow before continuing on. But the Flayer was unrelenting. Pursuing us through the twisted, burning streets, attempting to cut us off at every turn.

"Where to?" Lady Grey said as we ran into an intersection.

"Left!" I yelled, dropping back slightly to help Darkmist defend against the Flayer.

The left turn took us down a small alleyway. Cramped, making it difficult for the Flayer to teleport through. He resorted to teleporting onto the roofs above us, which gave us all the time we needed to make it to...

"The control tower! Over there!"

We pushed through the front doors, locking them behind us. The Flayer slammed against them, cut off mid-teleport. His burning blade streaked and slashed against the iron door. It held. For now. Behind us, a ship's wheel sat in front of a giant map. A red dot blinked Skytown's position, a short distance away from a massive ocean.

"I'll drive, you fight," Lady Grey stepped towards the ship's wheel. With the pull of a few levers, the room lurched and shook. No, wait, the city moved. An unsteady start, yet it was gaining speed now. For a second I imagined what it must look like to the people below. A burning chariot speeding through the skies, like some man-made comet.

BANG! The iron door toppled, half-melted, as the Flayer stepped into the room. Quick as a thought, an arrow sped towards him. As if by instinct itself, the Flayer raised its sword, the edge pointing away from him. The arrow crashed into it, splitting in two and falling uselessly to the floor. A second later and he was gone.

A woosh of air caught my attention, and I ducked just in time to have the Flayer's sword sail over me. He brought it down, cutting through a portion of the map and leaving a trail of lava in its wake. I rolled from it, the burning magma evaporating moments after appearing. Just what monstrosity of a weapon was this?

Perhaps privy to what we were trying, the Flayer eyed Caitlyn next. Though only for a moment. He was brought crashing to the floor by Darkmist. Clang! Their two swords met, with Darkmist trying to turn the Flayer's own weapon against him. Woosh! The Flayer was gone. Behind Darkmist now. A quick strike and Darkmist was down, clenching his burning arm.

I matched the Flayer's weapon, preventing it from ending my mentor's life. The Flayer rumbled something from its covered lips, in that strange language. Our blades pushed against one another, practically equals, but I felt my strength slip from my very bones. My legs twitched and shook beneath me, as I was brought to one knee. I pushed back as hard as I could, yet doubling my efforts only left me weaker by the second. My breath short, my fingers failing to grip my blade.

Then, with a cutting swipe, my sword was knocked away. The Flayer shoved me against the wall, its cold, clammy hands wrapped around my neck. Oh Jeb, how it was cold. A chill seeped into my veins, muscles and my very bones. My teeth chattered against each other, threatening to shatter. My vision tunneled, leaving me solely with a view of my foe.

It leaned towards me, and for the first time, I understood this creature.

Its eyes burned with a duality. Two conflicting fires raging within them. One burned brightly, a shimmering flame that never wavered or sunk. Its fuel was hatred, and its tinder, malice. Behind it, another flame sparked, yet lulled and dimmed beneath the first. One of sadness, of regret. It confirmed something that had been lingering in the back of my mind this entire time.

The Flayer was a servant, just as much as the Flayed. Yet before I could try to reason with it, it leaned towards me.

"You... will... serve."

Behind him, I could see Caitlyn frozen to the ship's wheel, unable to act. Darkmist groaned, trying to stand but falling back to the floor. The deep freeze grew thicker, enveloping my entire body. My fingers struggled to move, my neck creaked and I felt myself sinking beneath a dark wave, hands dragging and pulling at me. I struggled. I fought. I pushed back against it, swimming for purchase. The Flayer growled, but I refused. Refused to become one of him. Refused to become part of his sick and twisted game. Refused to fall here and now a-

A shining glow emanated from inside me. A bright spark lighting the fuse of some epic powder keg. Flames doused the cold, turning it to slush and burning the Flayer straight out of my veins. He cried that terrible cry, and I took the opportune moment. I slashed upwards, catching the Flayer from hip to shoulder.

He screeched, vanishing in a blast of smoke and leaving me in control of my body once more. Legs still trembling, I used my sword as support, limping over to Darkmist and helping him to his feet. Caitlyn kept her focus, continuing to push the city onward. We hovered over the edge of a landmass right now, the ocean within sight.

"What was that?" Darkmist asked.

"I... don't know," I shrugged, "I think I managed to break his hold over me."

He looked at me skeptically, "No one has ever broken the Flayer's hold during that process... that's incredible. Whatever you did... I felt it. This resounding warmth. This glowing beacon that broke whatever effect the Flayer had on me. Let me tell you, Axel, even for a Silverblade you're something special."

I would have loved more time to take the compliment in. Yet that happy moment was silenced by a shout and a clang. Caitlyn stood over the ship's wheel, having taken an ax to it. She marched over to the map and repeated the gesture, destroying the panel.

"There," she huffed to a shocked Darkmist and me, "now the Flayer can't change the course of Skytown. She's going down, so we need to make it back to the airship before we sink."

"And the people?"

"They'll be fine once Skytown crashes," Darkmist reassured me, "the water will break them out of the Flayer's influence. But we gotta go."

As if to sound off our departure, two of the Flayed burst in through a shattered window. We fled the control tower, returning to the blazing streets. Even crouching was a chore now, the smoke reaching lower and lower heights. Darkmist lagged behind us, clutching his arm and hissing with each movement he made.

"Are you okay?"

"That was some weapon," Darkmist rubbed his shoulder, "I don't fancy getting hit by it again."

"We've got medicine on the airship, we just need to m-"

Ahead was what had been the landing platform. Now? Smoke and flames. We'd been too slow. The fires had reached our ship, which crumpled and warped beneath them. I scanned the platform for other vessels, but the scant few that remained were experiencing their own Viking's funeral.

We were trapped.

"DANG IT!" Caitlyn smashed her ax into the ground, "OF ALL THE ROTTEN LUCK!"

She proceeded to utter a few other choice words, which I won't be repeating here. Darkmist didn't join her. Rather, he was much more solemn, staring out at the skies above. As for me? Well, this adventure was always going to be dangerous, wasn't it?

Behind us, the Flayed arrive. In their ones and twos and tens of dozens. Lurching towards us with that possessed look upon them, crying out for our end. The Flayer floated above them, arms crossed, apparently content to let his own forces handle this fight.

"Can we take them?" I asked Darkmist, who shook his head.

"Not without harming innocents," he said.

"Then that only leaves us with one option, doesn't it?"

"You're as insane as ever," Caitlyn sighed, sheathing her ax, "we're nowhere near the water yet. Who knows if we'll make it?"

"Only one way to find out, right?"

"Well, if you two don't have any better ideas..."

Darkmist leaped off the edge. Caitlyn was close behind him, leaving me and the Flayed on the landing platform. The Flayer twitched his head, seemingly daring me to do it. I glanced over the edge, spotting the clouds just below us, and the holes Darkmist and Caitlyn had made falling through them. I hesitated, but then I remembered.

Being a hero is about risking your life, right?

I grinned.

I jumped.

Made in the USA
Columbia, SC
04 February 2020